"You're the most amazing woman I know..."

Cupping Annie's cheek in his hand, Gabe bent close and kissed her.

It was something he'd been thinking about since the moment they first met. How many nights had he imagined what it might be like to hold her in his arms, to be the one that she waited for day after day, to know that she loved him?

Her lips were soft and warm, and Gabe gently probed the crease of her mouth with his tongue, deepening the kiss. She moaned, then suddenly pressed her hands to his chest, pushing him away.

She stared up at him, and a heartbeat later her palm met his cheek, stunning him back to reality.

"You need to leave. Right now. Just go, please."

"Annie, I—"

"I don't want to hear it," she said, placing her hands over her ears and shaking her head. Her eyes flooded with tears. "Get out."

As he walked out of the shed, Gabe cursed himself. What the hell had he been thinking?

He'd just betrayed his best friend.

Dear Reader,

It's true that time does pass quickly when you're having fun. In August 1993, my first book was published by Harlequin, a story called *Indecent Exposure* written for the Temptation line.

Since then, I've written ninety more books, mostly for Blaze. Twenty-three years have come and gone!

I've lived in three different places, gained and lost countless pounds, said goodbye to sweet feline friends, blown up numerous computers and laptops and visited many story settings, both in person and via the internet. I don't know what's next for me, but I know it will be fun to find out. I hope you come along for the ride!

Happy reading,

Kate Hoffmann

Kate Hoffmann

Off Limits Marine

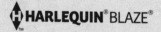

Recycling programs
for this product may
not exist in your area.

ISBN-13: 978-0-373-79970-1

Off Limits Marine

HARLEQUIN®
www.Harlequin.com

Printed in U.S.A.

Kate Hoffmann's first book was published by Harlequin in 1993, and in the twentysome years since, she has written ninety stories for the publisher. When she isn't writing, she enjoys genealogy, golfing and directing student theater productions. She lives in southeastern Wisconsin with her two cats, Winnie and Gracie.

Books by Kate Hoffmann

Harlequin Blaze

Seducing the Marine
Compromising Positions

The Mighty Quinns

The Mighty Quinns: Dex
The Mighty Quinns: Malcolm
The Mighty Quinns: Rogan
The Mighty Quinns: Ryan
The Mighty Quinns: Eli
The Mighty Quinns: Devin
The Mighty Quinns: Mac
The Mighty Quinns: Thom
The Mighty Quinns: Tristan
The Mighty Quinns: Jamie

To get the inside scoop on Harlequin Blaze and its talented writers, visit Facebook.com/BlazeAuthors.

All backlist available in ebook format.

Visit the Author Profile page
at Harlequin.com for more titles.

To Birgit, Malle, Susan, Marsha, Brenda, Adrienne and Johanna—for all you've done to make me a better writer.

Prologue

HE OUGHT TO be used to funerals by now. He'd been to enough of them over the years that he expected his grief to be numbed, reduced to a dull ache.

Marine Captain Gabriel T. Pennington drew a deep breath of the warm evening air. In the distance, he heard the sound of a fighter jet, taking off from Miramar, and he looked up at the sky, searching for the vapor trail in the late-afternoon light.

This was a different kind of grief, though. Deep and powerful, like a wound that wouldn't heal. He'd lost his best friend, a guy he'd known for a decade. And unlike the other funerals he'd attended, this one wasn't followed quickly by a return to active duty and the strange rhythms of a war zone to occupy his thoughts.

He cast his gaze across the wide lawn, his eyes fixed on an old shed set on the rear of the property. It had been two weeks since they'd laid Marine Captain Erik Jennings to rest and Gabe was still looking for something to ease the ache inside him. Perhaps this was it.

The shed door rattled as he drew it aside along a rusty runner. The light switch was beside the door and Gabe flipped it on, then squinted against the harsh glare from a bare bulb.

The familiar lines of the sleek wooden sloop were visible, even when hidden by the dusty tarp. He pulled the canvas cover aside, revealing a sailboat sorely in need of some tender loving care. Running his hand along the faded bright work, Gabe smiled to himself, remembering the late nights they'd spent working on the boat.

Erik had bought the old sloop with money he and Annie had received for their wedding five years before. He'd named it the *Honeymoon* and convinced Annie that one day he'd leave the military behind and sail her around the world. To most people, it might have looked like a lark, but to Erik and Annie, the boat had been an insurance policy, a promise that they'd have a happy future together, even if the military kept them apart.

Gabe and Erik had been friends since their plebe year at the naval academy. Ten years of friendship that had taken them to the far side of the world and back, Gabe as a Marine helicopter pilot based out of Camp Pendleton, and Erik as a Marine F-18 pilot out of Miramar, call signs Angel and Breaker.

They'd come from opposite coasts of the country, Erik from San Diego, the son of a surgeon and a socialite, and Gabe from Portland, Maine. His father was a lobsterman and his mother taught school. They'd arrived at Annapolis with two goals in mind—

graduating first in their class and nabbing a spot in Marine Aviation School immediately after that. Their choice of the Marine Corps had put them in the minority among the sailors at the naval academy, but it had bonded them as brothers.

Gabe had been Erik's best man at his wedding to Annie Foster, and now a pallbearer at his funeral. Was that full circle? he wondered. Somehow, it seemed as if Erik would never have a chance to finish his circle.

Death had become an accepted part of military life, at least at this point in time. And yet the loss of a friend, a subordinate or even a soldier he'd never met had become harder and harder to rationalize.

Erik had been doing what he loved. He was a patriot. He gave the ultimate sacrifice. All of the words rang hollow when Gabe realized that he'd never see his best friend again. They'd never share a few laughs over a beer. They'd never joke their way around a golf course or work late into the night on a moldy old sailboat.

"What are you doing out here?"

Gabe opened his eyes to find Annie standing in front of him. Her eyes were red and she clutched a wadded handkerchief in her hand. Even in her state of grief, she was more beautiful than he remembered. His fingers clenched with an instinctive urge to reach out and touch her, to smooth his hand across her cheek.

Gabe smiled and shrugged. "I just wanted to take a last look."

"Last look?" she murmured, then took a ragged breath. "You got your orders?"

He nodded. "This morning. I'm headed back to Afghanistan." Gabe forced a smile. He had always been happy to get his orders, to have a purpose to his life. But not this time.

Annie nodded. "It's time you get back to your own life. It's been two weeks. Although I've appreciated all your help with sorting and packing, I can get along fine on my own."

"I know you can," Gabe said.

"I'm glad you do, because I'm not so sure. I keep trying to catch my breath, but it just…hurts." She pressed her hand to her chest. "I'm trying to be strong, but I can't do it. I'm just so…angry."

"You're allowed to feel whatever you feel," Gabe said.

"It was a training exercise," Annie said. "Would I feel differently if he'd been shot down over Afghanistan? At least I'd have an enemy to blame. Who do I blame now?"

"It was an accident," Gabe said. "There's no one to blame."

"They think it was pilot error," Annie countered.

Gabe gasped, frowning as he met her gaze. "Is that what they told you? I hadn't heard."

"They've just started the investigation, but they warned me that the report might come back as pilot error. They wanted me to be prepared."

"No way," Gabe said, shaking his head. "Erik was a great pilot. He didn't make mistakes. He was a fanatic about safety, and there isn't another pilot in the

US Marine Corps who could pull himself out of an emergency situation better than Erik."

Annie dabbed at her nose with the handkerchief and nodded, his words seeming to bring her some sort of comfort. She slowly circled the boat, running her fingertips along the blue fiberglass hull. "Look at this raggedy thing," she said. "I must have been crazy to say yes when he told me he wanted to buy it." Annie looked over at him. "You wouldn't want to buy a sailboat, would you?"

Gabe shook his head. "I don't think so."

"I suppose I'm going to have to sell it."

"You've got some time to decide," he said.

Annie shook her head. "I have decided. I'm going back home," she said. "My parents asked if I wanted to take over the sailing school, and I said yes. There are just so many memories here, I'm not sure I could bear it."

Silence descended over the interior of the shed as she continued to circle the sailboat. As Gabe watched her, his mind wandered back to the very first time he laid eyes on her. He and Erik had a weekend pass and had wandered along the waterfront in Annapolis, only to find themselves in the middle of the victory celebrations for a sailboat race. Annie had captained the winning boat, and as was the custom, her crew had thrown her into the water.

"You looked like a drowned rat," Gabe murmured.

She glanced over her shoulder, and his heart stopped. The way the light framed her face, the soft wave of pale hair that fell across her cheek. Her beauty took his breath away.

"What?" she asked.

"What?"

She smiled winsomely. "You said something."

"I was just remembering the day you and Erik met. When he pulled you out of the harbor. You looked like a drowned rat."

Gabe had been first to step to the edge of the dock, offering his hand. But Erik had playfully shoved him aside and come to her rescue. It had been the genesis of their call signs, Breaker and Angel. Erik had been the bad boy, the heartbreaker, while Gabe had been his alter ego, the good guy who always did the right thing.

He'd always wondered what might have been if he'd done the wrong thing that day, shoving Erik aside and declaring his intentions to his best friend.

"Oh, yes. My hero. I was lucky he was there. You would have probably let me drown."

"I've always thought you were the kind of woman who could save herself," he said.

She opened her mouth to speak, then shook her head. "I hope I am," she said after a long silence. "I feel like I'm going under and I can't get back to the surface."

"Give yourself some time," Gabe said.

"This is nice," she murmured. "Talking to you. It's always been so…weird between us. I always got the feeling that you didn't approve of me."

"That's not true," Gabe said.

"I know it must have been difficult. You guys were best friends, and then I came along like a third wheel."

He couldn't tell her the truth. From the moment he'd first seen her, standing on the dock, soaked to the skin, he'd been smitten. She'd been everything he'd ever wanted, smart and funny and beautiful in a pure and natural way. Of course, Erik had moved first and used his extraordinary charms to lock her down. Within an hour of their first conversation, Gabe knew that there would be no reversal of her affections. Her heart belonged to Erik.

Gabe had never been jealous. Hell, he'd been happy that Erik had found a woman to love. At least that was how he'd felt until he realized that his best friend wasn't the best husband in the world.

Erik had always been a flirt. He seemed to thrive on the attentions of beautiful women. But when a guy got married, all the extracurricular activities was supposed to stop. At least that was what Gabe had always believed. But Erik had kept right on, with a girlfriend in every port. They'd argued over it twice and for a while Gabe had thought it might be the end of their friendship.

Five years later, Gabe wasn't sure if he'd ever given up the girls. Erik stopped confiding in him. And when they went out, he was friendly to the ladies but left alone at the end of the night. They simply never spoke of it.

"I should get back to the house," she murmured. "Erik's parents are coming for dinner and— You wouldn't want to stay, would you? They love having you around." She glanced over at him. "I like having you around. Right now, I'm having a hard time dealing with them."

"Why is that?"

"They asked me the other night if there was any chance that I might be pregnant. I can hear the disappointment in their voices. It was my duty to provide a grandchild, and I didn't get it done." Annie shook her head. "I...I'm sure they'll want to say goodbye before you leave."

Annie stared into his eyes, and he could see the tears begin to fall down her pale cheeks. Gabe didn't know what to do. They'd been talking about dinner, and suddenly tears. What could he say?

At a loss, he reached out and gently pulled her into his arms, holding her close as she wept against his chest. This round of tears seemed to be much worse than the previous few. Her tears soaked the front of his T-shirt, her fingers clutching at the faded cotton.

"It's going to be all right," he said softly.

"You'd think I'd be out of tears by now," she whispered. "I think I'm finally done crying, and then I realize I'm all alone. He's not coming back."

"You're not alone," he said. "If you need anything, you can always call me." He smoothed his fingers over her cheeks, wiping away the tears. "You'll be all right. You're strong and you're smart. You're the most amazing woman I know."

Annie frowned, and Gabe cursed inwardly. He'd gone too far. He'd revealed too much. He wanted to turn and walk away before he made any further mistakes. But instead, he let his heart overrule his brain. Cupping her cheek in his hand, he bent close and kissed her.

It seemed like the only thing left to do, something he'd been thinking about since the moment they first met. How many nights had he imagined what it might be like to hold her in his arms, to be the one that she waited for day after day, to know that she loved him? And how many times had he flown a mission wondering if his last chance might be taken away by an enemy RPG or a laser-guided missile?

Her lips were soft and warm, and Gabe gently probed the crease of her mouth with his tongue, deepening the kiss. She moaned, then suddenly pressed her hands to his chest, pushing him away.

Sometimes, a guy didn't get a second chance. Gabe knew that better than anyone. Hell, Annie knew it, too. You had to seize the moment. No regrets. And yet, by the look on her face, all that Gabe could feel was regret.

She stared up at him and a heartbeat later her palm met his cheek, stunning him back to reality. Gabe opened his mouth to speak, but she held out her hand to stop him.

"You need to leave. Right now. Just go, please."

"Annie, I—"

"I don't want to hear it," she said, placing her hands over her ears and shaking her head. Her eyes flooded with tears. "Get out."

As he walked out of the shed, Gabe cursed himself. What the hell had he been thinking? He'd spent his whole professional career as a pilot making decisions based on a cold, rational assessment of a situation. It had kept him alive in a dangerous world. And now, the first time he'd ever listened to his heart, he'd managed to screw the pooch.

He'd never see her again. She'd remember this moment forever and always hate him for it. He'd betrayed his best friend, and now he'd be left to suffer for it.

1

ANNIE JENNINGS ADJUSTED the delicate lace wedding veil, watching the reflection in the mirror. "Perfect," she murmured.

"Where did you find it?" Lisa asked.

"Packed away in my closet at home. It was my great-grandmother's. My grandmother wore it and so did my mother." Annie sighed. "I was stubborn and thought it looked too old-fashioned, so I chose my own veil. But I knew you'd love it. You've always appreciated vintage things more than I have."

A warm breeze fluttered at the lace curtains of the old farmhouse. Outside, in the pretty orchard, the guests were assembling, ready to witness the wedding of Captain Jacob "Nellie" Maranello and Annie's best friend, Lisa Romanoski. The rural setting in coastal North Carolina was perfect for a sunny Saturday in early June.

"Are you sure you want me to wear it?" Lisa asked. "Maybe you'll want to wear it someday."

Annie shrugged. "Maybe. Maybe not. Maybe I've had my one great love. Who says I'll find another?"

She carefully spread the veil behind her friend. Lisa was the only military "wife" she'd kept in touch with after Erik's death. Erik had served in Jacob's squadron, and they'd been stationed together since flight school at Pensacola. Jacob had also been in Erik's class at the academy, though he'd spent two years in Afghanistan before being accepted to the academy.

Annie grabbed a small bag from the bed and withdrew a faded velvet box and held it out to her. "Here. This is something borrowed."

"The veil is borrowed," Lisa said.

Annie shook her head. "That's something old. Your dress is new. This is borrowed and..." She pulled a garter out of the bag. "This garter is blue."

"I am not going to wear a garter. I may appreciate vintage things, but I'm definitely not a traditional bride. And we are certainly not going to do that horrible garter thing."

"You certainly aren't traditional. You and Nellie have three kids. You make your own yogurt. Your children are named Sky, River and Breeze. You're serving tofu at your reception, and I don't think you own a pair of shoes that aren't Birkenstocks. But you can bow to this one tradition. For your matron of honor?"

Rolling her eyes, Lisa yanked up her skirt and pulled the garter over her bare foot. Then she took the velvet box from Annie's outstretched hand. She

opened it to find a pair of diamond chandelier ear-
rings in a platinum Art Deco setting.

"I remember these," Lisa said. "I helped you put
them on at your wedding."

"My grandmother gave these to me along with
the veil. They'll go perfectly with your dress and
your hair."

Lisa gave her a hug. "I love them. Thank you." She
bent closer to the mirror and put them on, then turned
to show Annie. "What do you think?"

"The most beautiful bride in the world," Annie
said, her eyes filling with tears. She couldn't help but
remember her own wedding day. All her dreams and
hopes tied up in a white dress and veil. "Sorry," she
murmured, turning away from Lisa to busy herself
with her own jewelry.

Lisa sat on the edge of the bed, a frown of concern
etched across her brow, then patted the spot beside
her. Annie reluctantly joined her.

"I'm crying because I'm happy for you," Annie
said.

"It's been over a year," Lisa said.

"One year, five months and about sixteen days. I
know how long it's been. Believe me, I've felt every
one of those days."

"I want you to have fun today. Dance and laugh
and drink too much. Find yourself a handsome man
and flirt a little bit. Maybe even kiss him."

"I want to do that. But I just feel like I'm betray-
ing him. Like it's too soon."

Lisa gave her hand a squeeze. "You can't go on

like this," she said. "He would have wanted you to be happy."

"I know. And I've been thinking about what's been holding me back. It felt like there was something unfinished between us. And I finally realized what it was. The *Honeymoon*."

"I thought you never had a honeymoon."

"We didn't. We got married and he left for basic two days later. But I was talking about the boat. The sailboat he bought with our wedding money. We were going to sail around the world with it."

"That wreck you keep in your boathouse?" Lisa asked.

"It's not a wreck anymore. After I had it trucked out here from San Diego, I decided to spend some time fixing it up. And it's almost ready to sail. In a few months, I'm going to sail it to California. And if that goes well, I may just decide to keep going."

Lisa shook her head. "California? So you're just going to sail on down to the Panama Canal all by yourself. What about hurricanes? What about pirates and drug runners and…and whales? Whales run into sailboats all the time. Haven't you read *Moby Dick*?"

"I'm well aware of the dangers," Annie said. "I've been sailing since I was a kid. This is something I need to do. I think maybe it might be the closure I need. I'll take the honeymoon we never had, and then I'll sell the boat in California and come back here."

"Well, I think it's a crazy idea. If you want closure, you need to find yourself a new man. And there are plenty of handsome, single men invited to this wedding."

"And all of them are in the military," Annie said.

"My soon-to-be husband was in charge of that side of the guest list, so I can't be blamed. What's wrong with a military man?"

"I don't think I can go through all of that again. The waiting, the worrying. I just want a regular guy. An accountant or a salesman. Someone who will be home every night and doesn't have anyone shooting at him."

"I know exactly what you mean. That's why I refused to marry Nellie for so long," Lisa said. "I waited until he was done with active duty."

"You have three children," Annie said.

"I couldn't help myself. But now he's home and safe. It's the right time. The kids are old enough to start questioning why Mommy and Daddy have different last names. Nellie's got an engineering job lined up with Lockheed, and we're going to finally live a normal life."

A knock sounded on the door, and Annie went over to open it. Lisa's six-year-old daughter, Sky, waited on the other side. She was a bridesmaid and carried three bouquets in her arms.

"Grandma said I should bring these to you and that they're ready for you to come down."

She handed Annie a simple clutch of daisies and gave her mother a bouquet of white roses. Lisa gave her daughter a hug. "Do you remember what to do?"

Sky nodded. "I walk with Riv on this side and

Breezie on this side. And Riv carries the rings and Breezie throws the petals. And then we stand next to Annie and try not to squirm. And if we're good, we get to drink as much soda as we want to."

Annie laughed. "That's a nice reward."

"You dance with a few men, and I'll let you have soda, too," Lisa said.

"All right." Annie grabbed Sky's hand. "Let's go have a wedding. Are you excited?"

The little girl nodded.

"Me, too." They walked out into the hall, Lisa trailing behind them. As they reached the first floor, the rest of the bridal party was waiting. River and Breezie looked more nervous than excited, as did Lisa's father, John.

They arranged themselves on the back deck, taking last-minute instructions from Lisa, before they began their walk to the orchard. They were in sight of the guests when a dark-haired man in a blue Oxford shirt came jogging past them.

He turned and faced Lisa, his hands up, his expression contrite. "Sorry I'm late. You look great. Where should I go?"

"Gabe! We didn't think you'd make it."

"Change of plans," he said. He glanced over at Annie and for an instant their gazes locked. The smile faded from his face. "Annie? What are you doing here?"

She swallowed hard, unable to fashion a coherent reply. All that she could manage was a very meek "Hello."

He quickly turned and headed toward the gathering of guests. Annie let out a tightly held breath and tried to keep her whole body from melting into a puddle. How many times over the past seventeen months had she thought about that kiss? Too many to count. And every time it had come to mind, always in speculation of what might have happened had she responded, it had been followed by waves of guilt.

"What was that?" Lisa asked, looking back and forth between the retreating Gabe and her matron of honor.

"Nothing," Annie murmured. "I was just startled. I didn't know you were going to invite him."

"He's one of Nellie's buddies. Remember? He and Nellie were in flight school together."

"I remember. Erik, too." She drew a ragged breath. "I...I just haven't seen him since that night. You know, the kiss."

Lisa's mother grabbed her daughter's arm. "Darling, they're waiting. We need to go. We're already seven minutes late."

"They'll wait," Lisa said. She turned back to Annie. "What kiss?"

"Didn't I tell you about that?" Annie asked.

"No."

"Oh, I thought I had. Well, a few weeks after Erik's funeral, Gabe kissed me. In the boat shed. We were talking and I was crying and he was holding me and... it just happened."

"Darling, they've started the processional music. Everyone is waiting."

"Mother, I'm the bride. Nellie has been waiting all these years to marry me. Believe me, he'll wait a few minutes longer."

"I'm fine," Annie said. "We have to go." She took River's hand and gently drew him along. "Come on, let's go get married. Your mother and I can talk later."

"Damn right we'll be talking later," Lisa muttered. "I'm going to want all the details."

When they reached the far end of the aisle, Annie sent the children down, pointing to their father and their uncle Peter, who were waiting next to the minister. River chose to run, while Breeze took her job seriously, plucking one pink rose petal at a time from the basket and placing it on the ground in front of her. Meanwhile, Sky was forced to walk at a snail's pace behind her, rolling her eyes and urging her little sister to speed it up.

The processional music finished before Annie had even taken a step up the aisle, so to everyone's laughter, the vocalist began the song all over. Annie slowly walked toward the flower-covered arbor, her gaze fixed on the white ribbons as they blew in the breeze.

She knew he was watching her, but she was afraid to look around and risk meeting his gaze. If she had told Lisa about the kiss, then she could have written this off as a setup, pure and simple. They were best friends and she should have at least mentioned it. But Annie had kept that night a secret and, over time, tried to rationalize her response.

She'd been mourning her dead husband, she'd been emotionally overwrought, she hadn't been thinking straight. Her whole world had been turned upside down, and Gabe had offered her comfort in the only way he knew how—by kissing her. By kissing her?

Even she wasn't deluded enough to admit that the kiss wasn't about just comfort. There was an underlying passion, a need that couldn't be ignored. It had been the last thing she'd expected Gabe to do.

Since that unexpected moment had happened, she'd wondered what Gabe had been thinking. Had he been so crude to believe that now that she was a widow she was free to indulge? She couldn't come up with any other explanation. In all the time they'd spent together before Erik's death, he'd always seemed mildly annoyed with her, as if she were standing in the way of "bro" time with his best friend.

She clutched her bouquet more tightly, trying to focus on the job at hand. Just five more steps. Four. Three. Two. And stop. She slowly turned to watch the bride come down the aisle, flanked by her parents.

Maybe he'd been testing her. That was probably it. Testing her loyalty to her husband. What better place than after his funeral. Annie felt her anger rise. How dare he question her fidelity. After all, she was the one left behind all those times when Erik was deployed.

He was out fighting wars and doing his patriotic duty, while she was at home, worrying about him. And never once, not in five years of marriage, had she thought about straying. Never once had she regretted marrying Erik, even though they'd been miles apart for more days than they'd been together.

She wouldn't be tempted by Gabe again, Annie mused. As far as she was concerned, there was nothing between them. He was her husband's best friend, but they had never had a relationship. She'd say hello, make polite chitchat and then leave him to his own devices.

She glanced over at him again and found him staring at her. He smiled, and Annie felt her stomach flutter. He looked good. He was even more handsome than she remembered. Oh, damn, this was going to be a lot harder than she could have ever imagined.

SHE WAS DELIBERATELY avoiding him. The reception was in full swing beneath an open-air tent at the edge of the orchard, people dancing to a country band after a meal of barbecue and burgers. Strings of lights crisscrossed the canvas above their heads, mimicking the stars that twinkled in the night sky. The mood was casual, and everyone was out of uniform and primed to party into the night. Hell, most of the guests were already well beyond their limit, but Gabe had decided to forgo the alcohol and keep his mind sharp and focused on just one thing—Annie. Oddly, every time he moved in to try to talk to her, she slipped away.

He was beginning to feel like some crazy stalker, but he'd decided the moment he saw her that he was going to find a way to talk to her, to apologize for what had happened that night in the boat shed.

Annie had danced with nearly every single guy at the reception and was dancing with Lisa and her kids when he decided to make his move. She was distracted and didn't see his approach.

"Hey, kids. Can I dance with you, too?"

"Uncle Gabe can always dance with us," Lisa said, reaching out to pull him into their circle. "Annie, you don't mind if he dances with us, do you?"

"Actually, I'm a bit tired. I think I'll go sit down and rest."

"No," Sky said. "Stay with us!"

"Yeah, stay with us," Gabe said.

Annie shook her head, then turned and walked off the dance floor. The three kids watched her leave, then gave Gabe a disapproving look. "She was tired," he said with a shrug.

"Maybe you should go after her," Lisa said.

"She's been avoiding me all day. She's so good at it, I'm thinking she might have gone through SERE training since the last time I saw her. Survival, evasion, resistance and escape. She's got evasion down."

"So go ahead and test her resistance," Lisa teased.

Gabe grinned. "We do have a lot to talk about."

"I'm sure you do. I'd start with that kiss."

"She told you about…"

Lisa nodded. "She sure did. Bold move, Captain Pennington."

"Stupid move," he said. "I need to apologize."

"Ask her to dance," Lisa said. "I'll go request a slow song, and you'll have four or five minutes to say what you need to say."

Gabe left the dance floor, more determined than ever to speak with Annie. She had to know that the kiss was just a simple expression of affection. He'd never meant to cause her a single moment of pain or regret.

He found her at the dessert table with a plate full of sweets. She watched his approach with a suspicious eye but didn't make a move to evade him. Gabe decided that humor was the best option, so he stood next to her and stared out at the dance floor.

"If that plate is too heavy, I'd be happy to hold it for you," he said.

"You once said I was the strongest woman you knew," she said. "Were you lying to me?"

"I wasn't referring to your biceps," he said. "And I think I said that you were the most amazing woman I knew."

"Are you sure about that?"

"Trust me," he murmured. "I remember every word we said to each other that day."

"Just the words?" she asked.

He turned to her, their gazes finally meeting, her eyes flashing with defiance. Gabe grabbed the plate from her hand and set it on a nearby table. The band began a soft country ballad, and he jumped on the opportunity. "Why don't we dance? It will make it much easier to talk. And it will burn off a few of those calories you were about to consume."

"Do we have anything to talk about?" Annie asked.

"I'm sure I'll find something," he said, taking her arm and leading her along. When they reached the dance floor, he slipped his arm around her waist and pulled her close. He'd never been much of a dancer, but he decided to do his best impression of Fred Astaire. "I'm going to start with an apology. I'm sorry about that night. I don't know what I was thinking, but I never should have kissed you."

"Why did you do it?" she asked.

He fought the urge to tell her the truth. That he'd been desperate, convinced that the moment between them might be the last they ever spent together. He was heading back into a war zone, and though he didn't want to think about dying, he couldn't help himself. For him it was a life-and-death decision, not the impulse of a horny Marine.

No, he wouldn't tell her the truth. He'd take a page out of Erik's playbook and let her believe that it was driven by some other form of desire.

"You know, I've tried to figure it out. I think I just wanted to make you feel better. Kissing is the only thing I know that always works with a weeping woman."

The explanation sounded silly and shallow. He added a crooked smile as she regarded him suspiciously, hoping that might sell it.

"You're speaking from your considerable experience with women?"

Gabe chuckled. "See? We're talking. That's a good thing. Do you forgive me? Because I am sorry. And I do regret my behavior that night. If you forgive me, we might be able to be friends. And besides being an excellent dancer, I'm an outstanding friend."

He could see her softening, and when she finally

smiled, he felt a surge of satisfaction. It wasn't over between them. He'd have another chance. And this time, he wasn't going to blow it.

"Come on," he murmured, leaning closer. "You're not the type to hold a grudge."

"All right. I forgive you. But if you try it again, I might have to punch you."

"That sounds like fun," he teased. "I guess I have something to look forward to."

They continued to dance, leaving the banter behind and giving Gabe a chance to focus on the steps. It felt good to hold her in his arms, to feel her body sway against his. She was exactly as he'd remembered her—stubborn, feisty, opinionated. And sweet, funny and beautiful. All at the same time.

When the music stopped, she quickly stepped out of his embrace and clapped politely. "Thank you," she murmured.

"I haven't had any cake yet," Gabe said. "Would you like to join me? I think we left your plate over there." She opened her mouth to speak, but he placed a finger over her lips. "Before you say no, remember that we have a lot to catch up on."

"All right," she finally said.

They found an empty table, and he pulled out her chair and waited for her to sit. "Can I bring you anything else?" he asked. "Champagne? Or some punch?"

"Punch," she said. "No, champagne." She forced a smile. "I better stick to punch."

"I'll bring you both. Be right back."

Lisa and Nellie were standing near the cake table

as he stacked a few more pieces on Annie's plate. Each of the four layers was a different flavor, so he chose a variety. "Great cake," he said.

"Have at it, buddy," Nellie shouted.

Lisa sent him a knowing smile, as if she'd been watching the two of them. "Be nice," she warned, handing him a cold bottle of champagne.

He stopped at the punch bowl and balanced a cup on the edge of the plate, then returned to the table. He carefully set the plate in front of her. "I didn't know what flavor cake you liked, so I brought all of them."

She stared silently at the plate for a long moment and he realized that bringing her so much might seem like a comment on her eating habits. Jeez, when was he going to learn to think before he acted?

"Didn't you bring yourself a plate?" she asked. "What are you going to eat?"

He pulled out a chair and plopped down next to her, chuckling at the cool look she cast his way. "I thought we could share." Gabe speared a bite of carrot cake, then popped it in his mouth. "Good cake. So, how have you been?"

"Good," Annie replied. "Most of the time. The sailing school is doing pretty well. We had a record number of students register for the summer. I had to build a new bunkhouse. We added a couple more programs and brought in some great mentors for the students to work with. But it's never going to make me rich."

"I'd like to stop by and see it," he said.

She gave him a sideways glance. "Why would you want to do that?"

"You rent boats. I might want to go sailing. I'm going to be moving to the area in a few weeks. I've been temporarily assigned to do some consulting on new avionics software at Pax River. I'm going to be working with Nellie."

"So you're making a career of the Marine Corps?"

"That's always been the plan. Unless NASA comes calling. I'm thinking I'd like to fly the new space shuttle."

"You have some big dreams," she said. Annie picked at her cake, then set her fork down and pushed the plate away. "Can I be completely honest with you?"

Gabe nodded. "Absolutely."

"If you're thinking there might be something between us, you need to know that I'm never going to be with you. I've decided that I need to find a man who isn't in the military."

"Yeah, that's a good idea. There's just one problem with that."

"A problem? What problem?" Annie asked.

"I'm in the military. And you already like me. I guess, if we're going to hang out, you're going to need to change your plans. I mean, you might just start to think of me as more than just a friend. I like to keep an open mind about things like this."

Annie shook her head. "You're very sure of yourself."

"When I see something I want, I don't stop until I get it."

"And what do you want?" she asked.

Gabe shrugged. "Lots of things. But a summer on the Chesapeake would be a good start."

Annie pushed to her feet. "I should probably get back to my duties as matron of honor."

"And I've got a long drive back to Pax River. It was nice talking to you again, Annie." He leaned over and brushed a kiss across her cheek. "I'll be seeing you."

He walked away from her without looking back, knowing that he was risking it all by playing it cool. Gabe wandered over to the bride and groom and promised that he'd be back for another visit now that they'd be residing on the same side of the country again.

When he leaned in to kiss Lisa's cheek, she wrapped her arms around his neck. "Don't give up on her," she said. "You two would be great together."

"I'll be seeing you next month," Nellie said. "Try to keep yourself out of trouble until then. I'm counting on you to make me look good to my civilian bosses."

As he walked out to his car, Gabe smiled to himself. He'd looked forward to reconnecting with a few old friends. He'd never expected to run into Annie Jennings. But he'd managed to piece together something that a simple kiss had nearly destroyed over a year ago.

"Mission accomplished," he murmured.

2

It was the end of the first camping session for sixteen-and seventeen-year-old sailors, and Annie was attempting to take a group photo with every one of the sixteen students and the four counselors on the deck of one of their J-22 sailboats.

The warm wind was brisk, blowing across the bay and kicking up whitecaps with each gust. Rigging clanked against the aluminum masts, causing a cacophony of noise.

"All right, settle down," she shouted. "Just let me get a few more, and then you can all go crazy. Joey, stand next to the mast with Alicia."

The older teens were fun to teach, and most of them had attended camp the previous summer, and Annie knew them well. They were already accomplished sailors, so they spent their mornings and afternoons talking about sail efficiency and racing tactics and heavy weather, their instruction based on their own personal interests.

"All right, campers, you are officially done. We've got a big lunch for you and your parents when they get here to pick you up. The six of you who are staying for the next session are also invited to the picnic. Any of you high school seniors who are interested in being a camp counselor next summer, please see me before you leave. I've loved having you all and hope to see you back next—"

She felt herself being propelled forward, and a moment later she was in the water with two of the college-age counselors. How they'd managed to get off the boat and sneak up behind her she didn't know, but it was part of the tradition at the camp on the last day of a session. Everyone took a dip off the dock.

After a few minutes of good-natured splashing, Annie swam to the ladder at the end of the dock. As she crawled up, a hand reached out to her and she took it, leaping up to put both feet on solid wood.

"Thanks," she said. But as she looked up, she realized that her knight in shining armor was Gabe Pennington. He was dressed in his everyday uniform, khaki shirt and navy pants, his cover dangling from his fingertips. Dark sunglasses hid his eyes.

"This looks familiar," he said. "Isn't this where we began?"

She smiled, pulling her ponytail to the side and wringing it out. "Do you want to go in?"

"No, ma'am."

Annie started down the dock. "I thought you Marines were good on both land and water." Annie glanced back at him. "What are you doing here?"

"Can't I come and visit an old friend?"

She laughed lightly. "Are we friends? I don't recall coming to a firm decision on that point."

"I've been looking for a place to live on the weekends, and there was a cottage for rent a few miles north of here. I thought I'd swing by and say hello while I was in the neighborhood."

Annie arched an eyebrow. It was bad enough having Gabe in the same state, but if he was going to be living just a stone's throw away, she wasn't sure she was comfortable with that idea. "How did it look?" she asked.

"It wasn't right for me," he said. "Too much yard work. And I need a place that's close to restaurants. I don't cook for myself, so there has to be some options close by. And a place to do my laundry. And work out. And I'd hoped to get something on the water."

"Sounds exactly like the base," she said.

He nodded. "Yeah, it does. But I'm going to live there during the week. I just like a place to get away."

Annie wasn't sure where the idea had come from or what compelled her to extend the invitation, but the words were out of her mouth before she could stop them. "You could always stay here," she said.

Since her parents had retired to Florida, she'd struggled with living in an empty house. Though the camp was usually filled with student sailors, Annie didn't socialize with them in the evening, leaving that to the college-age counselors. So instead, she'd been left to her thoughts, which she figured were much more dangerous than Captain Gabe Pennington.

"Here?" he asked.

"There's a small efficiency apartment above the old boathouse. But it's a mess and it needs some work. If you do the work, you can live there for free."

"I'm not really a handyman," he said.

"You helped Erik with his boat," she pointed out.

"Yeah, but I just did what he told me to do. Why don't you show me this place and then I'll decide?"

The sailing school was set on a beautiful piece of property on the western shore of the Chesapeake Bay. Her grandfather had founded the school after he had served in the Navy in World War II. Her father had taken it over a few years after her oldest brother was born. He'd offered the business to both of her brothers, but they'd made lives of their own in Seattle and Chicago and had no interest in an almost-failing business. So she was left to run the place on her own.

The boathouse sat near the water's edge, the lower story home to the *Honeymoon*. The shallow, sandy bottom on the western shore made it impossible to launch the sloop without trucking it to a deeper harbor, yet another cost to add to the ever-growing list for her trip. But she was almost ready to get wet and Annie was looking forward to that moment.

The upper story of the boathouse was a single room surrounded by windows that overlooked the water that the counselors sometimes used as a game room on rainy days. "There's something I want to show you," she said.

Annie led him to the lower floor, pulling open a creaky door. Light flooded in from the far end, and she flipped a switch to illuminate the bay even more. The *Honeymoon* loomed large in the cavernous space, resting in its timber cradle.

"Look at this," he said. Gabe reached out and pulled her into a friendly embrace. "I can't believe you decided to keep it. How did it get here?"

She'd stopped listening to their conversation and was focused on the feel of his hand on her shoulder. She'd been living off the memories of their last encounter, the dance they'd shared at the wedding.

"Annie?"

"What?"

"How did you get the boat out here?"

"I had it trucked across the country. It cost a fortune, but I just couldn't sell it. I wanted to finish it, for Erik. And for me. It's almost done. I've just got to put in the electronics and raise the mast and do all the rigging." She paused. "You could help me with that. If you'd like."

Gabe smiled and nodded. "I would like that. For Erik."

"I can talk about him now without crying," Annie said.

Gabe turned to face her, his hands resting on her waist. "I told you it would get better."

"That's why I'm going to sail it to California. I've decided it's the final thing I'm going to do for our marriage. He always wanted to sail across the Pacific, just the two of us."

"And who's going with you?"

"I'm going alone," she said. "I'm going to leave

at the end of August. If the boat isn't ready, I'll stop along the way and have the work done. It should be finished by the time I get to the Caribbean, and then it's a quick sail to Panama and then up the coast of Mexico to San Diego."

"You realize how difficult it is to sail north to California? You'll be sailing against the wind most of the way. And you'll have hurricane season on the East Coast. You're planning to leave at the worst time of the year. I don't think you've thought this out very carefully."

She'd been hearing the same thing from everyone she'd told. *It's too dangerous. There are hurricanes. How will you keep watch?* "I've heard all the cons," Annie said. "I'm an experienced sailor. I can handle whatever comes along."

"I think you're overestimating your talents. I don't approve. And I don't think Erik would approve either. And your parents certainly wouldn't."

She stepped back, avoiding his touch. Annie thought that Gabe, of all people, would understand what she was trying to do. "Well, luckily I'm a grown woman and I don't need anyone's approval. Besides, I need an adventure. I spent five long years sitting at home, waiting for my husband, wondering when our life was going to begin. And then he was gone, and all that waiting was for nothing. I need to go out and find my own adventures in life, not wait around for someone to bring them to me."

"Annie, this is dangerous for two people, let alone

one. Anything could happen out there. And no one would be able to help you."

"Of course it's dangerous. It wouldn't be an adventure if it wasn't a little dangerous. But maybe I need some danger in my life. Maybe I wouldn't feel quite so numb." Annie's anger went from a simmer to a boil. Who did he think he was? Sure, he may have helped her out for a few weeks after Erik's funeral. And maybe they had agreed to be friends. But what right did he have to make decisions about how she ran the rest of her life?

"Maybe it would be better if you didn't stay here," she murmured. "I…I have work to do. You know the way out."

With that, she turned on her heel and strode out the door. As she walked back to the office, she realized that the parents were starting to arrive for the last-day picnic. She'd have to paste on her friendliest smile and pretend that everything was just fine.

"Annie!"

"Go away," she shouted. "I can't talk now. I'm too busy."

"You don't look busy to me," Gabe said.

"Well, you don't know anything about me. I'm not surprised you think that."

Annie yanked open the screen door and walked into the kitchen, only to find the camp cook, Sarah Martin, hard at work on the lunch for the campers. Cursing to herself, she walked through to the front room, which was stacked high with boxes of

T-shirts and foul-weather gear, all imprinted with the school's logo.

She distractedly began to sort them. Hopefully, Gabe had taken the hint and headed for his car. But when she heard the screen door slam, she knew that the argument would probably continue.

Annie heard his footsteps in the hall, and a few seconds later he appeared in the wide archway. He stared at her for a long moment, then raked his hands through his hair. "You know, right after you and Erik got married, he took me aside and made me promise that if anything happened to him that I'd watch over you. And I agreed. And if I had married, he would have done the same thing for me. I take that promise very seriously, Annie."

"Well, I absolve you of your responsibility. Whatever promises you made are hereby canceled."

"It's not that simple," he said.

"Yes, it is. I'm going to make that trip, and you can't stop me."

Gabe crossed the room to stand in front of her. "All right, here's the deal. Over the next couple months, we're going to take the *Honeymoon* out on a series of shakedown cruises. We'll get the boat operating properly for a single-handed sailor, and I'll make sure that I'm confident that you can handle her in rough weather."

"I'm a better sailor than you are," she snapped.

"Yes, I know that. If everything is cool, I'll be waving goodbye to you from the dock."

It wasn't a bad deal, Annie thought to herself. She

was confident in her abilities as a sailor. And it would be nice to have some help in the shakedown phase, since there would probably be more than enough work for the two of them.

"All right," she said.

"We've come to an agreement?"

Annie nodded.

Gabe grinned. "All right, then." He glanced around the room. "Is there anything you need help with? I can give you a hand with the picnic. Or maybe put these boxes away."

"No, I'm fine."

Gabe reached out and took her hands in his, giving her fingers a squeeze. "There's nothing wrong with asking for a little help now and then." He slowly drew her hand up to his lips and kissed the back of her wrist.

Annie held her breath as a rush of warmth snaked up her arm. His dark hair had fallen across his brow, and she reached out and brushed it from his eyes. She could feel her heart beating in her chest as they stared at each other for a long moment.

"I should probably go take a look at that apartment," he murmured.

"Yes, you should," she said, letting her fingers drift down his temple and cheek.

Gabe turned into her touch and she froze, her fingers splayed on his jaw. Slowly, he bent forward and Annie knew that he wanted to kiss her. But after the last time, would he stop himself? Or would he give in to his impulse?

In the end, Annie decided to take things into her own hands. Pushing up on her toes, she wrapped her arms around his neck and gave him a long, delicious kiss. It had been over a year since she'd kissed a man with any type of passion. Her first kiss with Gabe had been so sudden she hadn't had a chance to figure out what it was all about.

But this kiss was different. She'd show him exactly who was in charge here. She made all the decisions in her life, including when to kiss him. Annie hadn't intended to let the kiss go on as long as it had, but now that they were well into it, she wasn't sure how to bring it to a graceful end.

Gabe's hands drifted down from her waist to her hips, and he held her there as he pressed her back against the doorjamb. Her body had gone from pleasantly warm to alarmingly ablaze in just a few seconds. She couldn't seem to catch her breath, and her knees felt like they were about to collapse beneath her.

"I should probably go," he whispered, his lips warm against her neck.

"You should," she said.

He leaned into her, his hips meeting hers in a provocative dance. "I'm going to go."

"Yes," Annie said. "Goodbye."

His tongue tangled with hers, leaving her lips damp with the taste of him. "Bye," he said.

Gabe lingered for a few minutes longer before he finally stepped away. His gaze searched her face, and Annie managed a coy smile. Though they'd both talked of friendship, it was becoming more than obvious that there was something more happening between them.

She drew a deep breath and waited for the guilt to assail her. But the only feeling she could manage was breathless anticipation. She liked kissing him and guessed that he felt the same way. And she enjoyed running those moments over and over again in her head.

In truth, she'd been spending far too much time thinking about Gabe and his handsome face and sexy mouth and killer body. There was definitely an attraction between them, Annie couldn't deny that any longer. So what had changed? Where had the guilt gone? Was it being overwhelmed by the excitement of the moment? Would it suddenly reappear and make her feel even worse for the thoughts that ran through her head?

Maybe if she spent a little more time kissing him, she'd be able to figure it all out.

GABE STOOD AT the end of the pier, staring out at the cluster of J-22s maneuvering around a buoy a half mile away. The wind was brisk but warm, and the bay had a scent that was so familiar to his senses that it brought memories swirling forth in his mind. As a kid, he'd worked his father's lobster boat and was well-acquainted with waters off the coast of Maine. But the Chesapeake was different, a spot where freshwater and salt water met. The shoreline was gentle and rolling with thick forests, so different from the rocky coastline of Maine.

A small motorboat ran alongside the sailboat race, and he could make out Annie behind the wheel. She was shouting instructions to the race participants as they tacked back and forth against the wind.

The more he got to know her, the more he found to admire. Everything she did, she did at one hundred percent, throwing herself headfirst into life as if she'd learned to appreciate every day.

It wasn't surprising, considering the loss she'd experienced. She thought her life had been perfectly planned ahead of her. It was impossible to fathom a future without her husband, so she'd never even considered it a possibility.

He'd only seen the marriage from one side, and he hadn't always liked it. But now Gabe was beginning to understand the other side, the fierce loyalty that Annie had toward Erik, the unconditional love that made it impossible for her to accept his passing.

It had been over a year since they'd shared that first kiss, and for the first time Gabe was hopeful that she was ready to move on with her life. Last weekend, she'd actually kissed him, and in the intervening days, Gabe had decided that her actions had been a definite sign. The attraction between them wasn't just one-sided.

In truth, he'd tried to keep things purely platonic, not willing to risk losing her over some silly torch he'd been carrying. But now things had shifted between them and he had cause to hope that there might be something more in their future. Sure, she'd been adamant about rejecting a man in the military. But could her views on that be softening?

He watched as the small motorboat split away from the sailboats and headed toward the dock. As she approached, he kept his eyes fixed on her, watching as her pale hair whipped around her face in the breeze.

She deftly pulled the vintage boat up to the dock and tossed him a line. "Get in. I'll take you for a ride."

"Don't you have to watch your students?"

"There's a counselor with each boat. They'll bring them in after the race."

He jumped in beside her, the line in his hand. "This is a really nice boat. You don't see too many of these anymore."

"My dad restored it. It's great for waterskiing." She pulled away from the dock and thrust the throttle forward. In a few seconds, they were skimming across the smooth surface of the bay, a soft spray coming up from the bow.

He closed his eyes and enjoyed the feel of the sun on his face. Gabe felt the boat veer to the left, and he opened his eyes and saw them approaching a spot on the shore. "Where are we going?" he asked.

"I wanted to show you something," she said. "When I was a kid, we used to come out here and play. It was like our own fortress. Take the line and go up on the bow. I'll pull it in close, and just hop out and tie us to a tree."

Gabe did as he was told. When the boat was secure, he held out his hand and helped Annie out. She started into the woods and he followed, wondering what she could possibly have to show him. Before long, they were hiking on a well-worn path, and up ahead he could see sunlight shining through the trees.

Birds sang overhead and the sound of the breeze ruffling the trees provided a pleasant counterpoint. A few seconds later they stepped into a clearing. Shafts of sunlight illuminated an abandoned stone church, the roof long ago caved in and the windows gone.

"Wow," he said, stepping inside the front doorway. Wildflowers grew up from where the floor used to be, and a rabbit skittered through the lush greenery. Vines hung from the walls, nearly obscuring the old windows. "What is this?"

"There was a settlement here, back in the 1700s," Annie said. "The whole village was burned to the ground when the church was struck by lightning. The people were too superstitious to rebuild, so they just scattered to other towns along the western shore." She walked along the wall and then found a spot. "Here it is."

Gabe stepped to her side and squatted to see some letters carved into one of the stones. "A.F. plus E.J. Annie Foster and Erik Jennings." Gabe smiled. "He told me about this. This is where he proposed to you."

Annie smiled and nodded. "It was really wonderful, but it didn't go perfectly. He set up a little dinner with champagne and candlelight. And then he came back to the house to get me. But by the time we got back, then sun was going down and the mosquitoes were vicious. And when we got here, a raccoon was sitting in the middle of the table, enjoying our dinner. All we had left was the champagne. So he got down on one knee and asked me. And that was that. We carved our initials in the stone and ran back to the boat, the mosquitoes chasing us the whole way."

"It's a good story," Gabe said.

"It is," she said with a wistful smile. "I always thought I'd tell it to our children and grandchildren someday." She walked over to one of the windows and stood in a shaft of light. "When I first got home, I used to come out here and talk to him. All the memories were so fresh and vivid and…perfect. I could still hear his voice." She sighed softly. "Now the memories are vivid, but they're also real. It's not just a romantic proposal anymore. Now the mosquitos and the raccoon are part of it."

"Isn't that the way it's supposed to happen?" he asked. "It helps you cope with your loss. Let's you move on."

"It's happening so fast," Annie said. Her voice grew soft and hesitant. "There are times when I can't remember him at all."

Gabe took a step toward her and reached out to place a hand on her shoulder. "You'll never forget him entirely."

"But he'll be replaced. Like he is now."

Gabe frowned. "What are you talking about?"

Her body trembled slightly, and she shook her head. "All I can think about is your hand on my shoulder. How good it feels to be touched again. How every time you touch me, even in the most innocent way, I seem to get all warm and breathless. My heart starts pounding, and the only person I can think about is you."

The confession seemed to take everything out of her, and for a moment he thought she was about to cry. Gabe drew her back against his chest and wrapped his arms around her waist, resting his chin on her shoulder. "What do you want me to do?"

Annie pulled out of his embrace, turning on him and holding her hands out in defense. "I don't know. I don't want to forget him. But the more time I spend with you, the harder it is." She forced a smile. "We should go. It's getting late."

"No, we should talk about this," Gabe insisted. "If this is going to be a problem, we can't just ignore it."

"Sure we can," Annie said with a laugh. She turned and scampered out of the old church.

Gabe followed her, stumbling through the thick brush. He finally caught her at the water's edge and grabbed her waist, pulling her back into his arms.

She stared up at him, breathless, the color high in her cheeks. He couldn't remember a time when she looked more beautiful, or more tempting. "Don't do it," she warned, her chest rising and falling.

He'd let it go for now, satisfied with the progress he had made. Gabe wasn't willing to risk her affection for a quick grope in the woods. He had a second chance; it would be foolish to waste it.

Gabe grinned, then took her hand and helped her back onto the boat. "This is going to be an interesting summer," he murmured.

THE SOUNDS OF a hot summer night drifted through the bathroom window—the quiet chirp of crickets, the far-off bark of a dog, the sound of the water lapping against the dock. Annie hung her leg over the edge of the tub as she sank into the cool water, closing her eyes and sighing softly. A fickle breeze teased at the lacy curtains, and she drew a deep breath, smelling rain in the air.

She swirled her fingers in the water, stirring up the scent of lavender, meant to soothe her nerves. Annie had tried to forget the fact that she hadn't seen Gabe in five days. During the week, he stayed on base. But on weekends, he was supposed to take up residence in her boathouse. It was now 11:00 p.m. on a Friday night, and he hadn't turned up.

With a soft curse, Annie sank beneath the surface of the water. She had no right to be irritated with him. And yet she was. Was it wrong to enjoy his presence? She was surrounded by teenagers without anyone to really talk to. Gabe was interested in her life.

She dragged the washcloth over her arm. To be honest, it wasn't just the conversation that she missed. It was the physical contact—the occasional touch of his hand that felt like a caress, or the warmth of his lips pressed against hers. She'd grown accustomed to the longing when she'd been married to Erik, but Gabe was different. With him, everything was new, more desperate, more intense.

They'd moved past the boundaries of friendship. The kissing and touching had burned that bridge. And yet she couldn't call their relationship a romance.

There was nothing of the typical trappings found in that kind of relationship—no flowers, no dinners out, no attempts at sweet gestures or flowery sentiments.

Instead, she felt as if she were caught in some no-man's-land, focused on the physical pleasures of his touch, yet determined not to fall in love with the man. This wasn't a romance, it was a…a fixation. An obsession. An infatuation.

She'd expected to feel guilty over her new fixation, but that feeling hadn't set in yet. Annie had been without a man for nearly twenty months. Any woman, widow or not, would be restless. And faced with easing those feelings with a man as sexy and handsome as Gabe, how could she resist?

Maybe it was time to move on, at least in the physical sense. She wasn't ready to fall in love again, and Annie wasn't sure that there was a man out there to replace her dead husband. But that didn't mean she couldn't move on physically, that she couldn't enjoy sex with another man. The physical contact would ease her loneliness, and when she was alone again, the memories would do the same.

Gabe was the logical choice. He was geographically available, he was physically attractive and, from all indications, he wanted her. They could indulge in a no-strings affair until she left on her sailing trip. The plan seemed remarkably simple. But how would she go about explaining her needs to Gabe?

After all the years of knowing him, he really didn't know her at all. How would he react if she dragged him into her bedroom and seduced him? A giggle bubbled out of her throat. Annie wasn't even sure how she would react. The thought of stripping his clothes off and pushing him back into the sheets sent a shiver skittering down her spine.

She drew a deep breath and waited for the guilt. But again, it didn't come. "Are you trying to tell me something?"

The last conversation she had with Erik was months ago. After he died, Annie used to speak to him all the time. But those things that used to soothe her had gradually faded in importance. She was thinking about sleeping with another man. "Gabe," she murmured.

An uneasy sensation washed over her. There it was. Guilt? Or was it indecision? She was lusting after her husband's best friend. Certainly, there had to be something immoral about that. Annie pushed out of the water and grabbed a towel from a nearby rack, wrapping it around her damp body. She took another towel for her hair, then walked out of the bathroom to her bedroom, leaving footprints on the wood floor.

This didn't have to be so complicated. They were both adults and they both had desires—desires that they could mutually satisfy. There'd be no doubts or regrets. And she'd get what she'd been so desperately longing for. The touch of a man's hands on her body. The warmth of his kiss and the overwhelming sensation of feeling him move inside her.

Annie let the towel slide off her body and puddle around her feet, then slipped into a faded cotton robe and tied it at the waist. She walked to her dresser, where an old fan whirred softly, and pulled her damp hair up off her neck to let the air dry her skin. Staring at her reflection in the dresser's mirror, she brushed the robe off her shoulder, revealing the soft flesh of her breast, the nipple barely covered.

Annie couldn't help but wonder if she even had the courage to act on her impulses. Seducing a man in her head was far easier than doing it in real life.

"I was wondering if you'd still be up."

The sound of his voice startled her, and she pressed her hand to her chest, clutching at the front of her robe. "I thought you'd decided to stay on base." She slowly turned, letting her hand drop to her side. Her robe gaped open provocatively.

It was a bold move, but well calculated. If a glimpse of her barely covered naked breast wasn't enough to lure him closer, then a full-blown seduction was nothing but a fantasy.

He observed her for a long moment, his gaze drifting down her body, then back up to her face. A tiny smile quirked at the corners of his mouth. "Do you have any idea how beautiful you are?"

She didn't know how to answer a question like that. Annie had never considered herself a beauty. In truth, she'd always thought she was rather ordinary. "Am I?"

"From the first time I saw you, that day on the dock, I've thought it."

She smiled. "Love at first sight?"

Gabe nodded. "Yeah. Absolutely. Love at first sight."

It was a simple declaration of his affection, but his words hit her like a slap to the face. Was Gabe Pennington still in love with her? None of this would work if there were actual emotions involved. She wanted a man for her bed, not for her heart.

Annie reached for the front of her robe, drawing it closed, then tightening the tie at the waist. "And you're still in love with me?"

He laughed and shook his head. "No! No, not at all." Gabe paused, then gave her a sheepish smile. "Well, maybe a little bit."

The atmosphere, so charged just a few moments ago, had shifted. "I...I should really get to bed. The kids are sailing in a regatta tomorrow, and they leave really early in the morning."

"Mind if I tag along?"

Annie was surprised by the offer. Spending an entire day with race-crazed teenagers wasn't for everyone. But she had to admit that she could use the help. Trying to keep an eye on sixteen rambunctious kids usually proved too much for the counselors. "Are you sure? These kids can leave you exhausted."

"No, it'll be fun. And I get to spend the day with you."

"All right," Annie said. "I guess it's a date. We leave at 6:00 a.m."

"All right, I'll see you then." He turned away from the door, then stopped short. "I brought you something. I left it down on the kitchen table."

"What did you bring me?"

"Nothing special. Just some of those almond croissants you like from that coffee shop in Annapolis you mentioned."

Annie frowned and shook her head. "When did I…"

"Last weekend. You were talking about buying doughnuts for breakfast and just mentioned the place. I remember stopping there with you and Erik back in the day. I was close by, so I decided to see if it was still there."

Annie laughed softly. "How is it you're still single? You'd think some woman would've snatched you up by now."

"You'd think," he agreed.

"You could possibly be the perfect boyfriend."

He gave her a shrug. "Now, if only someone were looking for the perfect boyfriend. Most women are looking for imperfection. I guess that's my problem." With that, he turned and walked back downstairs, his footsteps retreating through the house. Annie heard the kitchen screen door slam behind him, and she flopped back on the bed.

Closing her eyes, she let her memories wind back to that day on the dock. She remembered noticing him, his steady blue gaze, his shy smile. What had made her gravitate to Erik instead? How would life have been different if she'd taken Gabe's hand that day?

She'd still have a husband. Or had fate made that decision? Was everything a matter of fate? Erik hadn't been a perfect husband. There had been times when she'd doubted his fidelity and when she'd questioned the depth of his love for her.

So much of who he was was wound around his career as a pilot. He lived his life fueled by adrenaline, and when he was home with her, he was like a caged animal, restless and edgy. They'd often fight, but then he'd switch gears and turn on the charm and she'd fall for him all over again.

Groaning, Annie covered her eyes with her hands. Why was she suddenly questioning her marriage? Ever since Gabe had kissed her, she'd begun to see things differently. She'd begun to see *herself* differently.

Annie rolled off the bed and slowly walked to the dresser. She had tucked the envelope beneath a stack of her grandmother's embroidered handkerchiefs. From what she understood, every soldier wrote a letter meant to be delivered in the event of his death. Annie had received the envelope and read it once, then promptly tucked it away, unable to read through her tears. After that, there never seemed to be a right time to look at it again—until now.

The envelope was right where she'd left it, slightly crumpled and stained with tears. She sat back down on the bed and ran her fingertips over the writing that was once so familiar. These last few weeks, she'd been so consumed with thoughts of Gabe, she suddenly felt the need to be close to Erik again.

Annie walked to the overstuffed easy chair and sat, tucking her feet beneath her. Sliding her finger beneath the flap of the envelope, she held her breath, not certain she was ready to face the emotions within.

They'd fought the last time they were together. She'd finally told him that she was fed up with living her life alone and asked him to leave the Marines once his tour was up.

Erik had tried his best to appease her, but she had been intractable. She wanted him to make a choice, yet he refused. So they'd parted in anger. He'd called a day later to smooth things over, but Annie still wasn't ready to let go of her resentment. And then it was over and she was left with no choice but to live with those feelings.

Annie unfolded the letter, drew a deep breath and read softly.

"'My dearest darling,'" she murmured. "'I've never been one for flowery words and romantic sentiments, but know that I have loved you from the moment we met, and if it's possible, I will keep loving you in the hope that we will meet again someday. I know I haven't always been the perfect husband, but you've been the perfect wife. Don't spend too much time mourning me. There are plenty of men out there who will fall madly in love with you the moment they take your hand and look into your eyes. Live your life, find someone to love and all will be well again. I promise. My love forever, E.'"

Annie drew a ragged breath and slipped the letter back into the envelope. He was giving her permission to move on, to build a new life with a new man. There was no need to feel any guilt.

That still didn't solve all her problems. Finding the right guy was the key. And Annie wasn't sure whether Gabe was a proper candidate. He already felt it was his place to boss her around and offer opinions when they weren't welcome. And he nearly admitted that he was in love with her. The last thing she needed was a lovesick Marine trailing around after her, trying to talk her into marriage. He was a nice guy—maybe too nice.

Indulging in an affair with Gabe might be convenient, but it was also dangerous. She'd just have to decide how much danger she was willing to risk in a pursuit of immediate gratification.

3

THE ANNUAL Annapolis Yacht Club Youth Sailing Regatta was already in full swing when they arrived at the waterfront. Gabe helped the campers get the four boats into the water and rigged while Annie set off in search of the racing schedule.

He hadn't realized it until now, but this was the regatta that had brought Annie and Erik together. He remembered that he and Erik had just finished their third year at the academy, and they were hanging around to take a summer course when they spent the weekend wandering the waterfront in search of excitement.

And excitement they'd found. Lots of food and drink. Pretty girls with long legs and suntanned skin. Guys who were distracted by their race preparations. And sunshine and fresh air. It had been a perfect day, just like today.

"Are they all unloaded?"

He turned to find Annie standing behind him, her

eyes hidden behind a pair of horn-rimmed Ray-Bans. She wore a T-shirt emblazoned with the name of her sailing school, and Gabe fought the urge to pull her into his arms and run his hands over that incredible body. Instead, he forced a smile. "All set. Rigging has been checked and double-checked. They're just waiting for the race schedule."

Gabe watched as Annie waded into the crowd of campers and passed out copies of the schedule. She quieted them before going through a list of instructions, and when she was finished, they did a quick camp cheer before scattering.

When she returned to his side, she gave him a bright smile. "Let's go find some breakfast," she said.

"Don't you have to stay here and watch?"

Annie shook her head. "The counselors are in charge. And they have my cell phone number if they have any emergencies."

"The coffee shop with the almond croissants isn't too far from here."

"I ate that whole bag of croissants last night. I don't think I could eat one more."

"There were four in the bag," Gabe said.

"I was having trouble sleeping."

"I didn't sleep very well either," he said. "I had a lot of things on my mind."

She glanced over at him. "Like what?"

There were moments when he knew he ought to play it cool. And then there were other times when he just wanted to be honest with Annie and lay his feelings out on the table. "I was thinking about you...

dressed in that robe with your hair all wet. What was keeping you awake?"

"Guilt," she said.

It wasn't the answer he'd hoped for. "You feel guilty? About what?"

She shook her head. "I don't want to talk about that right now."

They walked along the waterfront in silence for a while, then found a coffee shop with tables overlooking the water. A waitress took their order and Annie chatted about the wind and the race conditions until the woman returned with lattes and cinnamon rolls.

"Do you think you'll get married again?" Gabe asked.

Annie drew a deep breath and considered the question for a long moment. "I don't know. I try to imagine my future, but I can't. That's why I want to sail the boat to California. I'm hoping if I make the trip we always talked about that I can finally figure it out."

"I don't understand you," Gabe said. "It's like you're carrying around this guilt. Where does that come from? You have nothing to be guilty about."

"I know," Annie said. "Maybe it's not guilt anymore. It's… Oh, I don't know. Confusion. I'm at loose ends." She swallowed hard. "I kissed you just after the funeral. I know he was gone, but he really wasn't. In my mind, I was still a married woman, and you were still his best friend."

"So you're going to risk death and drowning in a sailboat just to pay for some betrayal you feel over a simple kiss. What about all the kisses we've shared since then? How about that one you laid on me the other day?"

"That was curiosity," she said. "It's coming on two years. People keep telling me that it's time to move on. You're the only man who wants to kiss me, so I thought I'd take advantage."

"So I'm just an experiment?" Gabe asked.

"No," she said. "Maybe, a little. I don't really know what I'm doing. Don't expect me to explain myself."

"I'm beginning to realize that," Gabe said with a soft chuckle. He took a slow sip of his coffee, then set the cup down in front of him. "Do you ever wonder what would have happened if I'd pulled you out of the water that day after the regatta? Would it have been me?"

She gave him an odd look. "Did you want it to be you?"

"Yeah," Gabe admitted. "At the time, I did."

"I…I didn't know that. Why didn't you ever say anything?"

"I figured you ended up with the right guy."

She nodded. "I did," she said.

"Yeah, you did," Gabe lied. "But he's gone now. And I have a chance to pull you out all over again." He held out his hand across the table. "It's up to you whether you grab it or not."

She rested her fingertips in his palm and stared at their joined hands. "This is what I miss. Late at night when I can't sleep. The warmth of a touch. Sometimes, I just get so lonely." She drew her hand away and he noticed a tremble. "Is…is that something you could help me with?"

For a long moment, Gabe wasn't sure that he heard her correctly. She wanted something from him, but what it was couldn't be more unclear. Annie was lonely, and she needed him to touch her. But was that where it stopped or did she expect them to move on to other, more intimate acts? "I'm not sure I understand what you want," he said.

Annie groaned softly and covered her eyes with her hands. "Don't make me ask again. It was hard enough the first time."

"All right," Gabe said. "Why don't I just stumble around here until I figure it out? You can raise your hand when I get it right." He paused as he put his thoughts together, knowing that the conversation was full of land mines. "Can I assume that you want to change the terms of our relationship?"

Annie nodded. "Yes, that would be correct."

"You'd like me to be more…physical?"

She nodded again.

"More romantic?"

This time Annie shook her head. "Romantic wouldn't be bad," she explained. "But I can't fall in love with you. We need to make that very clear from the start."

"So sex is good, but romance is bad."

"Not bad," Annie said, "just unnecessary."

"Is there some reason you couldn't fall in love with me? I mean, besides the fact that I'm in the military."

She toyed with her napkin, avoiding his gaze. Impatiently, Gabe reached out and hooked his thumb beneath her chin, forcing her eyes up to his. "If you really want to do this, then we have to be honest with each other. No games. No lies."

"All right," she said. "If I fall in love again, I want it to be with a man who will be there for me. I want to see my husband every day, and I want to sleep with him every night. And if we have children, I want to raise them together. I fell in love with Erik so quickly, and I was so young, that I didn't really think it through. What it would be like for me. Our whole marriage revolved around his career—where he'd be stationed, when he'd be deployed, how long it would be before we saw each other again. I was a good military wife. I never complained. But if there is going to be a next time, then I deserve more."

Gabe had never once considered that Annie had been unhappy in her marriage. But listening to her words, he could tell that the time apart had taken a toll.

"I know that might sound selfish," Annie said, "but I need to start thinking about what's right for me. I'm going to finish up this season at the sailing school, and then I'm going to sail to California on the *Honeymoon*. After that, I'm not sure what I'll do. But I know that I'm not going to sit at home waiting for my life to begin while the man I love is out there living his."

There it was, Gabe mused. She couldn't have made it any clearer. The future that he imagined with Annie wasn't anything that she would ever want. So where did that leave him? Was he willing to live by her terms? Would it be enough? And if it wasn't enough, would he have the strength to walk away?

"It's an interesting proposition," he said. "And I understand your…dilemma. But I promised Erik that I would watch out for you. I'm not sure he would approve."

"He doesn't have to approve," Annie said, an edge of anger in her voice. "This is my decision. It's my life. And it's what I want."

"Why me?" he asked. "Why not find some other random guy? Some guy who doesn't love you."

Annie cursed softly. "Stop saying that! You don't love me. You barely know me. And I chose you because I trust you. You're here for the summer and then I'll be gone and then you'll be gone and it won't be complicated."

"You have this all figured out, don't you?"

She laughed softly and shook her head. "Not really. This could all blow up in my face." She reached out for her coffee and took another sip, her hand still trembling. "You don't have to give me an answer now. Think about it and let me know."

He didn't need time to think about it. And he didn't care what she had to say. He'd take the relationship on her terms and then do everything he could to change it to his terms. She might not want to fall in love now, but given time, he could persuade her to change her mind. And he'd start right now.

"There's just one thing," he murmured.

"And what's that?"

He stood and circled the table, then picked up her

chair with her in it and turned it to face him. Then he bent down, bracing his hands on the edge of the table, trapping her until she was forced to turn her face up to his. His gaze lingered on her lips for a long moment before he moved in to kiss her.

He didn't think much about what he was doing, just letting desire and need take over. He drew his tongue along the crease of her lips, and when she opened them, he took advantage, deepening the kiss until she moaned softly. His hand found her cheek, and when he drew away, Gabe ran his thumb over her damp lips.

"No holding back. We go at this full throttle or we don't do it at all."

Annie couldn't seem to manage a proper answer. Instead, she just nodded. It was enough for Gabe to see that even with all her rules and requirements, she wasn't immune to his touch. She might not want romance, but he sure as hell wasn't going to settle for anything less.

She would fall in love with him. He'd make sure of that.

"You have to watch them every minute," Annie said, holding the screen door open for Gabe. "They are teenagers, and teenagers go looking for trouble."

"They're just having fun," Gabe said. "Besides, where would they get booze? The counselors wouldn't buy it for them."

"Not if they wanted their jobs back next year," Annie said. She set the empty bags of snacks on the counter and then gathered the empty soda cans and began to crush them. "I understand they're celebrating. We won big today. I just think a few of them seem a bit more...jovial than normal."

Annie had been on edge since they'd returned from the race two hours ago. She'd spent the long ride back thinking about the conversation she'd had with Gabe and trying to convince herself that it was a completely rational move. But the more she thought about it, the more she realized how crazy it must have sounded. All the rules she'd laid out and for something that should've come naturally between them. She knew Gabe was attracted to her. So why not let it unfold on its own? Why did she have to be the one in control?

The more Annie thought about it, the more she wanted to rescind her offer. Or had it been a command? Whatever it was and however it came across, it was hanging between them now, like a big, dark rain cloud. He hadn't touched her since the kiss at the café, even though he had plenty of opportunities. Maybe her blunt proposal had turned him off. Like Erik, Gabe was a pretty traditional guy. A woman calling the shots was probably something rare in his world.

"If it will make you feel better, I'll go line them up and pat them down. If I find any suspects, I'm trained in advanced interrogation techniques. I'll be able to get the truth out of them, but I'm not sure where I'll find the bamboo to put beneath their fingernails."

"Ha-ha. Very funny," Annie said. "I don't think you're taking this very seriously. These kids are my responsibility. And while they're here, I have to keep them safe."

Annie watched as Gabe strolled over to the refrigerator and grabbed a cold beer. He twisted off the cap and took a long drink. "Maybe you should have a beer. You need to relax."

Shaking her head, Annie tossed the dish towel aside and walked to the door. She pushed it open and stepped out onto the back porch, letting the door slam behind her. Fighting the impulse to scream out loud. There were moments when Gabe acted so much like Erik, they might have been twins.

Erik had never taken her concerns seriously, no matter what they were. Whenever she was upset, he'd tease and joke until she either laughed along with him or stormed out of the room. Obviously, Gabe had no idea what it was like to be responsible for other people's children.

Annie clenched her fists and headed toward the group of kids gathered around the bonfire.

She didn't say a word as she walked through the crowd, grabbing Zach and Jeremy by the arm as she passed and dragging them toward their cabin. "Give it to me," she said. "You know it's against the rules, but if you hand the alcohol over right now, I won't send you home."

The boys glanced at each other, and Zach shook his head. She glared at Jeremy, and he finally shrugged and reached in his back pocket to produce a small bottle of vodka.

"Is this it?"

"Yes," Zach said.

"No," Jeremy said. "Give her the pot."

With a muttered curse, Zach reached in his back pocket and produced a small plastic bag.

"Where did you get this?" Annie asked. "Did you get it in Annapolis?"

Zach shook his head. "Naw, David brought it from home. He gave it to us before he left last week."

"And that's the end of it? There's no more?"

This time they both shook their heads. Annie pointed to the cabin. "Get to bed. I want you both up at 6:00 a.m. I've got some chores for you to do. And you make sure to let the other kids know if they have any contraband that they better turn it over to a couselor or risk my wrath."

When she got back to the kitchen, Gabe was sitting at the table, reading a sailing magazine and finishing his beer. She set the vodka down and put the plastic bag in front of it. "I told you so," she said.

"Booze and pot? That's a big score. So did you throw them in the brig or tie them to the keel? Keel-hauling is such an underrated punishment."

"You think this is so funny, but it's not. They know the rules. I could send them home." Annie grabbed a glass from the dish rack and poured herself a glass of lemonade. "They need to follow the rules. That's all I ask."

"They're teenage boys. And once in a while, they like to bend the rules, or maybe even break them. You could let it pass."

"That's funny coming from you. You live your life by rules."

He shrugged and took another sip of his beer. "And when there aren't any rules to follow, I just fly by the seat of my pants."

Annie groaned, pressing the cold glass of lemonade to her forehead. "Why are we arguing?"

"I think you're frustrated," Gabe said. "Not with the kids, but with me. You're wondering when I'm going to kiss you again or if I'm going to kiss you again, and you're tired of waiting."

Annie shot up from her chair, sending it screeching back over the linoleum floor. "I should have never said those things to you. I thought I could trust you, but you've turned it into some kind of game."

Gabe slowly stood and stepped toward her. "Isn't that what it is, Annie? There are so many rules. If you want me to seduce you, then we need to throw away all the rules." He took another step toward her and then another, and when he was close enough, he slipped his arm around her waist and pulled her body against his. "Too many rules requires too much thinking. And I don't want to think. I just want to feel." He smoothed his hand along her hip, then ran his palm upward to cup her breast. Gabe flicked his thumb over her nipple, quickly bringing it to a peak through the soft fabric of her dress. He bent closer, as if to kiss her, but then drew back, just as their lips were about to touch.

He continued to tease, with his touch, with his lips, with the soft sound of his voice in her ear. Annie felt her knees go weak. She'd forgotten how powerful his touch was. How had she ever thought that she could be the one in control? The minute he pulled her into his arms, her whole body betrayed her.

When he slipped his hands around her waist again, she thought he was finally going to kiss her. But instead, he picked her up and set her on the edge of the kitchen table, drawing her knees up along his hips and pushing her back until she was lying flat on the surface.

Slowly, he worked on the buttons down the front of her sundress, opening them one by one and exposing her from collar to waist. When they were all undone, he pushed the cotton bodice aside and pressed his lips to the skin along her collarbone. Annie felt her pulse quicken as he moved lower, his fingers tugging at the lace of her bra.

It had been such a long time since she felt the sensations pulsing through her body. Annie reached out for the hem of his T-shirt and tugged it over his head. She'd seen him without a shirt before and had only imagined what the muscle and bone would feel like beneath her fingertips. Now, as she ran her hands over his torso, she felt the muscles ripple beneath her touch, his skin alive with warmth.

"Is this what you wanted?" he whispered.

"Yes," Annie replied. It was exactly what she wanted and yet so much more than she expected. Erik had always treated sex like sport. Good exercise and great fun. But Gabe was different. He was focused and intense, as if his only goal was to please her.

He grinned, then kissed her again. "Good. Then we're on the same page." Gabe straightened, then grabbed his T-shirt from the floor. He tugged it over his head and raked his hand through his hair. "I had a nice time today," he said.

Annie pushed up on her elbows, frowning. "Where are you going?"

"To bed. I'm beat. I'll see you in the morning."

"Wait. I...I thought that you'd—"

"Sleep here?" His grin widened. "I'm not that kind of guy."

She watched as he walked out of the kitchen. The screen door creaked, then slammed, and Annie cursed out loud. She crawled off the table, then walked to the door and locked it. If he decided to change his mind in the middle of night, he wasn't getting inside. She wouldn't give him the satisfaction.

As she trudged up the stairs to her bedroom, she thought this all seemed like such a good idea twenty-four hours ago. She was finally taking control of her life and making her own choices. She was demanding what she needed and determined to get it. But instead, she felt as if her life were careening out of control, and Gabe Pennington was the cause.

He was just a man, a man she barely knew. But since the moment he'd kissed her, she hadn't been the same. Annie walked into the bathroom and turned on the water for the tub, sitting on the edge as she tested the temperature.

When it was as cold as she could stand, she stripped off her clothes and slipped into the water, the chill shocking her nerves. She felt overheated, as if every nerve in her body were on fire, generating an unbearable heat.

Annie closed her eyes and let her head drop back on the edge of the old tub. An image of him flashed in her mind, and she groaned softly. Locking the doors might have been an overreaction. Maybe she ought to leave them unlocked—just in case.

"CAPTAIN GABE PENNINGTON. I was hoping I'd run into you today."

Gabe twisted in the pilot's seat and saw his buddy Nellie Maranello standing on the tarmac. "What the hell are you doing here? I thought they only let real pilots on the base."

"Aw, you know me. The smartest pilot in the Navy. They weren't going to let me get far before dragging me back in."

Realization slowly dawned and Gabe shook his head. "I was wondering how I got this assignment. Did you put me up for it?"

"I wanted the best," Nellie said. "For fixed wing, that's me. For rotary, it's you. To be honest, it was that report you wrote on the problems with the T-scan software. I heard the higher-ups were pretty damn impressed. I had very little to do with it."

Gabe had thought it was just pure luck that had brought him to Pax River. Now he knew there were other factors at work. But he'd never expected his report to be read by anyone beyond a few quality-control geeks in the aerospace industry. These kind of things could drag a military career to a dead halt if they weren't welcome by his superiors.

Gabe switched off the electronics, then crawled out of the pilot's seat and jumped out of the chopper. "So you are just interested in my technical expertise?"

"Nah, I just wanted to look at a pretty face every day. When I take you out for a beer after work, I know all the prettiest girls will be hanging with us."

Gabe felt his jaw tighten and his temper flare. "Goddammit, Nellie, you're a married man. Why would you risk that just for a little tail?"

"Hey, I was kidding. You know I don't mess around. It took me ten years to get Lisa to marry me. I'm not going to screw that up now."

Gabe drew a sharp breath and nodded. "All right, then. We're not going to have any problems." He grabbed a clipboard from the rack and made a few notes, then glanced up at Nellie, who was watching him with a curious gaze.

"Do you want to tell me what that was all about?" Nellie asked.

"Not really."

Nellie glanced at his wrist. "It's almost four o'clock. What do you say we knock off and get ourselves a drink? We can start the real work tomorrow. Once you have a few beers, I'm sure you'll explain yourself."

"There's nothing to explain."

"I'm sure we'll find something to talk about," Nellie teased, clapping Gabe on the shoulder. "Did I tell you that Lisa is pregnant again? Number four. I'm thinking we'll just keep going until I have a base-ball team."

As they strolled out of the hangar into the late-afternoon heat, Gabe glanced over at his friend. "How do you make it work? You two spent so much time apart. Lisa had to raise the kids on her own, and yet here you are, perfectly happy. How is that possible?"

Nellie shrugged. "I don't know. I guess I just picked the right girl. She does her thing and I do mine. And we do the family thing together." He glanced over at Gabe. "I heard you've been spending week-ends with Annie. Is that what caused your outburst?"

"Where did you hear that?"

"My wife tells me everything I need to know. And she insisted that this was something that I needed to know."

They hopped in Nellie's car and made their way to the officers' club on base. It was only a short drive to the sprawling brick building that sat on the water's edge. They grabbed a couple of beers at the pub, then headed out to the patio to enjoy a late-afternoon breeze.

Though Gabe wasn't one to broadcast the details of his personal life, he was glad to have Nellie to talk to. The situation with Annie had him confused and on edge, and he wasn't sure about his next move. A guy like Nellie might have some insight.

"So I guess you decided to break the bro code."

Gabe looked up from his beer to find his friend studying him intently. "The way I see it, he's the one who broke the code first. I saw her first. I pointed her out, and we went over to meet her. Then he just stepped in front of me."

Nellie chuckled. "Yeah, that's Breaker all right. He never did follow the rules."

"I think he managed to break almost every rule when it came to women." Gabe glanced over at Nellie. "You know what I mean?"

"You're talking about his…extracurricular activities? I think most guys were aware of what was going on."

Gabe winced and shook his head. "That guy never appreciated what he had. Does Lisa know?"

"She's the one who told me. For a while he didn't take much care to hide it."

"But she's never mentioned it to Annie?"

"Maybe you should," Nellie said.

"How would that even go? I mean, how does one bring up the subject? Oh, by the way, your husband cheated on you through most of your marriage. She'd hate me forever. Hell, she'll probably hate me if she finds out I've known all along. Either way, I can't win."

"You really are hung up on her. What's the problem?"

"Besides the fact that she thinks her late husband was perfect? Or that she doesn't want to marry another guy in the military? Or that she only wants to use me for sex? Take your pick."

Nellie held his hands out. "Whoa, whoa, whoa. Go back to that third one."

"Yeah, that's the one that's got me confused, too. She doesn't want to get romantically involved, but I guess the physical relationship is just fine. I thought I understood women, but this makes no sense. And then there's this whole thing about sailing to California. In a few months, she's going to hop on an old boat, sail to Panama during hurricane season and end up in San Diego."

Gabe tried to rub the knot of tension from his neck. He had less than forty-eight hours before he saw her again, and all these questions still needed answering.

"Listen," Nellie said. "You face life-and-death situations every day when you're deployed. This isn't going to kill you. Just make a decision and move forward. Military tactics."

"How am I supposed to explain what—"

"No!" Nellie said. "No explanations. You don't have to say a word. Show her what you want. You're a man of action, not words. Just keep your mouth shut and do what needs to be done."

Gabe glanced at his watch. If he left now, he could be back to Annie's place before supper. They'd have the whole night together, and he could drive back to the base in the morning. "What time are you and I meeting tomorrow morning?"

Nellie grinned. "Make it nine. That will give you plenty of time to drive back."

Gabe drained the rest of his beer and then stood. "Thanks, Nellie. I appreciate the insight."

"Don't put too much trust in my advice," he said. "Remember, it took me ten years to get Lisa to marry me."

Gabe left Nellie nursing his beer on the patio. He

grabbed a passing shuttle, which took him back to the barracks. This assignment was a nice break from an overseas deployment. His schedule was flexible, and though he reported to superiors, he had a lot more freedom to come and go as he pleased. But he'd always felt more at home in a battle zone. He liked the tension, never knowing what was going to happen in the next minute or hour. He was protecting lives, and nothing was more important.

Here, back in the United States, he felt like a fish out of water. He needed a whole different skill set to survive. It wasn't about nerves and focus. Here, he had to maneuver in unfamiliar territory.

Romance was much more complicated than war, Gabe mused. There were land mines everywhere, and bombs falling out of the sky. But it was way too early to surrender.

Gabe pulled his cell phone out of his pocket and considered his next move. He could text Annie and let her know that he was coming, maybe suggest that he pick up something for dinner along with a good bottle of wine. Or he could surprise her and catch her off guard.

He wasn't sure exactly where he stood with her, but by the end of the night he'd know.

4

ANNIE SAT ON a small stool in the examining room of the local hospital's ER. She watched as a young doctor stitched up a gash on Zach Wilson's forehead. His best friend, Jeremy Porter, watched from the other bed, his hair still damp.

"Does he have a concussion?"

The doctor shook his head. "Except for the cut, he seems to be fine. From what I hear, these two were lucky."

Annie drew a shaky breath and nodded. In truth, she was the one who was lucky. The accident could've been a lot worse. Her family's sailing school had an excellent safety record, which would now be spoiled by two reckless teenagers. "How long will it be before they can leave?" Annie asked.

The doctor glanced at her. "We'll want to watch them for a few more hours, just to make sure they're all right."

Annie stood and nodded. "Fine," she said. "I'm

going to go call your parents and ask them what they'd like me to do."

Jeremy groaned. "Do you have to call them again? After the pot and grass thing, they grounded me for three months. They're going to be so pissed I'll be grounded for a year."

"And I get hurt like this all the time." Zach pointed to a long scar on his arm. "Stitches are nothing. Don't call them. Don't send us home."

Annie pulled a curtain aside and walked out. As she got to the hallway, she heard a commotion near the nurse's desk. A few seconds later, she recognized the tall, lean form of Gabe Pennington. He was dressed in his flight suit, a khaki-colored jumpsuit that hugged his long limbs and broad shoulders.

She called his name and he turned, a look of concern etched across his features. He crossed the distance between them in a matter of seconds and wrapped his arms around her. "Are you all right?" He drew back, holding her face between his hands as he made a quick examination.

"What are you doing here?" Annie asked. "How did you know where to find me?"

"When I got to the house, I couldn't find you. One of the counselors came up and told me that you were at the hospital. That there had been an accident. I came right over."

"It wasn't me," Annie said with a smile. "It was a couple of the boys. Zach and Jeremy. The ambulance brought them here, and I followed."

"Then you're okay?"

"Yes. And they appear to be fine, too, although that may not be the case after I call their parents. Again." Annie suddenly felt exhausted, so she walked to a nearby chair and sat. "I just don't understand these kids. Their parents pay all this money to send them to sailing school, and they risk getting sent home for some stupid prank."

Gabe sat beside her and draped his arm around her shoulders. "You do a great job with these kids."

"No, not a great job. I just barely keep up. Running the school is really a two-person job. My parents did it, my grandparents did it. I'm barely making ends meet. It's a two-person job and I can't do it alone."

"Send them home," Gabe said.

"I don't really want to do that. They're here on the four-week program, and I know their parents would probably demand a refund."

"You have a refund policy?"

"Yes. No refunds. But they've been sending their kids for years. And I—"

"No refunds. Stand firm." He gave her shoulder a squeeze. "You'll be fine."

Annie shook her head. "Will I? The property taxes on the sailing school are enough to sink me. Twenty-five acres along the water in one of the wealthiest counties in the country. Never mind all the upkeep for the buildings and the boats. The school just barely breaks even. After that, there's nothing left." She closed her eyes and tipped her head back. "I never thought to look at the books before I accepted the job.

My parents never let on that there were problems. They always seemed so happy."

"You're a clever woman, Annie. You'll make it work."

"This property has been in my family for years. I can't be the one to lose it."

"I can help you," Gabe offered. "I have plenty of spare change and nothing to spend it on. I'll invest in the school."

Annie was stunned by the offer. She hadn't been fishing around for a loan; she was simply blowing off a little steam. But now, knowing Gabe, he wouldn't be satisfied until she accepted help from him.

"I still have Erik's death benefits," she said. "I've been saving that for my trip, but it's enough to pay the taxes."

Annie couldn't help but wonder what it might be like to have Gabe in her life full-time. Even with Erik away most of the time, Annie had still been aware that he was looking out for her. If something went wrong, he'd been available by phone to help, even though he was thousands of miles away. It was easier to face the world as a pair, rather than a single.

"Annie, you can't be afraid to ask for help. There are plenty of people in the world who care about you and will step up."

She pushed to her feet, ready to put a close to the subject. "I don't know what to do about those two," she said. "First the drinking and the pot. Now this. They could have both drowned before anyone had a chance to get to them. Thank God one of the counselors saw what happened and was right on top of things."

"What happened?"

"They decided to take a small catamaran out. I told them it was too windy, but they sneaked out anyway. They were sailing into the wind and had the thing heeled over as far as it would go while they were both in harnesses dangling off the other side. They lost control and they both went in, without life jackets I might add. Zach hit his head on the boom and cut it open. Jeremy got caught in the sails and nearly drowned." She drew a ragged breath and glanced up at him. "I'm almost tempted to call their parents from here and have them pick them up right from the hospital."

"Have you talked to the boys?" Gabe asked.

Annie shook her head. "I doubt it did any good. They just don't want me to call their parents."

"Would you like me to talk to them?" Gabe asked.

"As much as I'd love you to go all deranged drill sergeant on them, I think I have this covered."

He wrapped an arm around her shoulders and pulled her close again, pressing a kiss to the top of her head. "Give them to me for a day. I'll find some work for them to do around the school. They'll be so busted that they'll be a couple of angels for the rest of their time at camp."

At this point, Annie was willing to try anything. To a pair of sixteen-year-old teenage hooligans, Gabe could be pretty intimidating, especially dressed in that flight suit. "Thanks," she said. "I think I can take care of it."

Annie leaned into his body, thinking to herself what a great father he'd make someday. She'd always had a hard time thinking of Erik as a father. He seemed to be more of a child himself, and he'd happily delayed talk of starting a family. But the more she saw of Gabe, the more she began to understand that he had a much different approach to life. He was more serious, more focused. He knew exactly who he was.

"I've always wanted to try keelhauling," he murmured. "Sounds like a real good time."

Annie laughed softly. "I prefer walking the plank. It's much tidier." She craned her neck to peer into the examining room. "I wonder how much longer we'll have to wait."

He slipped his hands around her waist and stared down into her eyes. "Come with me," he whispered. Gabe grabbed her hand and pulled her along the hallway, peeking into windows as they passed. When he found what he was looking for, he pulled open the door and gently steered her inside before following her.

It was dark, but she heard the lock click behind her and an instant later his hands were cupping her face and his mouth was on hers. He seemed desperate to taste her, and his tongue plundered again and again until she surrendered completely. And she didn't want to fight him. It felt so good to just let go and to enjoy the power he held over her.

Her heart pounded in her chest and she could barely catch her breath. The taste of him made her dizzy, and she tightened her grip in an attempt to stay upright. Someone tried the door, rattling the knob, but they couldn't get in.

"We can't stay here," she murmured.

"Just a few more minutes," he pleaded, his lips finding the pulse point on her neck.

Annie felt as if she'd lost the ability to refuse him. Isn't this what she'd wanted all along? For some reason the fantasy was nothing like reality. In her mind, it was all so polite, so controlled. But what was happening now was the opposite. They were careening down a hillside with no way to stop.

His hands were all over her body, his palms smoothing along the length of her torso, then drifting up to cover her breasts. She felt hot, as if the room were closing in on her, and she tugged at her clothes, desperate to cool her skin.

When she reached for the hem of her T-shirt and began to pull it up, Gabe grabbed her wrists and pinned them on the wall above her head. Annie was trapped, with no way to move, and she twisted against him, their hips grinding provocatively.

Gabe groaned and finally let her wrists free. But Annie didn't feel any sense of relief. Instead, she grabbed the front of his shirt and shoved him against the wall. As he continued to kiss her, he found tempting new locations, spots on her body that were particularly sensitive to the touch of his lips.

Through the haze of passion, Annie heard a voice above her head. It was the hospital's PA system, and she immediately turned her attention away. But a few seconds later, she heard her name. Turning aside, she listened, trying to ignore the heat from his lips on her collarbone.

"Paging Annie Jennings. Please report to the ER nurses' station. Annie Jennings to the ER nurses' station."

Annie spread her fingers across his chest and pushed Gabe back. "They're calling me."

He looked down at her, his eyes still glazed with desire. "Calling you?"

Annie hurriedly began to straighten her clothes. She ran her fingers through her tousled hair and then drew a deep breath. "You stay here," she said. "Don't come out until after you've counted to one hundred."

He reached for her again, but she brushed him away, then slipped out into the hallway. When she reached the nurses' station, the doctor was waiting there, clipboard in hand. Annie pasted an apologetic smile on her face. "I'm sorry," she said. "I just went to find something to drink."

"We're going to keep the boys another hour, and if there are no problems, they can go. If you'd like to call their parents, I'd be happy to talk to them and give them a complete rundown on their health."

Annie glanced over her shoulder, but Gabe hadn't emerged from the room. "That would be fine." She followed the doctor down the hall, and they sat on a pair of chairs. She tried to focus her thoughts, but her mind kept returning to what had happened in that room.

She couldn't help but wonder what would come next. Would they go back to her place and continue on with what they'd started here? A shiver skittered down her spine at the thought. The anticipation was more than she could bear.

"Are you all right, Ms. Jennings? Your face is flushed. Do you feel faint?" the doctor asked.

"I'm fine," Annie said. "It's just been a very long day." And if things went as planned, the night would be even longer.

THE HOUSE WAS silent when Annie and Gabe walked in. The campers had waited up to see if the boys were all right and welcomed them back with open arms. Annie was still angry. She asked them all to grab their camp chairs and gather around the fire pit.

Gabe stood on the back porch and watched them for a while. She'd called the parents from the hospital, the doctor speaking to them about the medical conditions of both boys. And now she was reading the campers the riot act for the second time since Gabe had arrived.

From the look of her, she was emotionally exhausted. He opened a bottle of wine and poured two glasses, then walked upstairs. He hadn't made any specific plans for seduction, but Gabe had decided he was going to take a slow approach.

They had the rest of the summer to get to know each other, and he didn't want to move too quickly and scare Annie. He took a sip of wine, and as he passed the bathroom, he had an idea of how to begin.

He started by filling the bathtub, adding some of the bath salts that she kept on a shelf above the faucet. He managed to find a few candles to create a relaxing atmosphere, then grabbed some fluffy towels from the closet in the hall.

He stretched out on the floor of the bathroom and was enjoying his wine when he heard her come in and call his name. "I'm up here," he shouted. A few seconds later he heard her footsteps on the creaky wood stairs, and then she was standing in the doorway of the bathroom. The outline of her body was illuminated by the candlelight.

"What's all this?" she asked with a coy smile. "You've been busy, I see."

He handed her a glass of wine, and she sat beside him on the floor, her slender legs stretched out in front of her. Gabe reached over and ran his hand along her thigh. It was a simple caress, but it sent a powerful current through his body.

"About this plan of yours," he said. "I've been thinking, and I believe we should just let this progress at a very careful pace. That way, we're both sure that it's the right thing to do."

He continued to draw his fingers up and down her thigh, tracing designs on her skin and occasionally drifting down between her legs. She seemed focused on his touch and at first didn't reply to his proposal. "So, is that all right with you?" he asked.

Annie blinked, then looked over at him, a frown wrinkling her brow. "What?"

"Would you rather take it slow?"

"Well, yes, slow is nice. But sometimes fast is

good, too. Or even…medium. Does that answer the question?"

Gabe took her wineglass from her fingers and set it on the tile floor. Then he grabbed her hands and pulled her to her feet. "Why don't you get in the tub? I'm going to go down and get dinner."

"You brought me dinner?"

"I brought us dinner," Gabe said. He turned to her and grabbed the hem of her T-shirt, then pulled it up over her head. He'd intended to get her started, but when Gabe saw the scrap of her bra against her tan skin, he decided to take some time to appreciate what he'd uncovered.

His gaze fixed on her chest, her perfect breasts barely covered with satin and lace. Reaching out, he slipped a finger beneath the strap, gently tugging it off her shoulder. When the other side was done, he looked at the clasp between her breasts.

Over the years, through many midnight fantasies, he'd tried to imagine this moment. The fantasies had always been accompanied by a good measure of guilt. He was lusting after a married woman—the wife of his best friend. It wasn't technically cheating, but there were times when it sure felt like it.

Now was not one of those times. He was finally free to look at her and touch her and believe that at some point in the future they could be together.

Gabe held his breath as Annie opened the clasp. A moment later the bra slid off her arms and dropped to the tile floor. He felt like some silly schoolboy, his heart slamming in his chest, his mind reeling with the possibilities of what might happen.

All of his senses were on high alert. He could hear the crickets outside and the voices of the students shouting at each other in the still night air. The drip of the faucet and the sound of Annie's deep, even breathing. He watched her chest rise and fall, wondering what was going through her head.

"You can touch me," she murmured.

He'd been with his share of women in the past and knew exactly what came next. But something held him back. He didn't want just her body. He wanted her heart and soul, her mind, her love. He wanted everything that made her who she was. Could he settle for just her body?

Impatiently, Annie reached out and grabbed his hand, spreading his fingers across her left breast. Heat snaked through his body, pooling in his lap. He couldn't resist any longer. Cupping her flesh with his palm, Gabe bent down and pressed a kiss to the rosy tip.

Annie drew in a sharp breath as if surprised by the sensation of his lips on her nipple. Her fingers slipped around his nape and she pressed him closer, her hand smoothing over her other breast.

It took every ounce of his determination to keep himself from stripping her naked and taking her right then and there. But this was Annie and she deserved more than just a quick fuck and mutually satisfying orgasms. He'd waited all these years. A few more hours wouldn't hurt.

Gabe drew back, smoothing his hands around her waist. "I'm going to go down and get our dinner," he murmured. With that, he turned and walked out of the bathroom, his hands clenched at his sides. There were so many ways this could go wrong that Gabe was almost afraid to make a move.

But to win a woman like Annie, Gabe knew that he might have to take risks. He wanted her to know the depth of his feelings, especially if they were going to make love. But Annie was determined to keep him at arm's length. Should he just be honest? Or should he hide his feelings until she was ready to accept them?

The Chinese food he'd picked up on his way home was still wrapped in brown paper, sitting on the kitchen table. He untied the string and pulled out the cartons, opening them as he went along. Some old memory had told him that she liked Chinese food, but he wasn't sure of the particulars, so he bought a little bit of everything.

He grabbed a couple plates and forks and carried the Chinese food up the stairs. He found her sitting on the floor next to the tub, wrapped up in her robe, her bath untouched. Gabe handed her the food and then plopped down beside her.

"I hope you're hungry. I bought one of almost everything. You know how it is with Chinese food. So hard to decide."

Annie grabbed the first box and peered inside. "Sesame chicken? And what's this?"

"Sha cha shrimp. I didn't know whether you liked spicy."

"I love spicy."

"Fork or chopsticks?"

"Chopsticks, please."

"Soy sauce?"

Annie shook her head.

They spread the food out on the floor in front of the bathtub, an odd little picnic for two. "We really don't know that much about each other, do we?" Gabe commented. "I don't even know what kind of Chinese food you like."

"I hate egg drop soup," Annie added.

"But for two people who are about to sleep together, we don't know a lot more."

Annie picked through the box of General Tso's chicken, then pulled out a plump bite and popped it in her mouth. "Does it really make a difference? I mean, we're only going to be together until the end of the summer, and then we'll go our separate ways."

"It sounds so simple," Gabe said, shaking his head.

"Isn't it?"

Gabe searched for the words to explain how he felt, but he'd never had to say them out loud before, he'd never had to justify his beliefs about life and love. "Life is short," he murmured. He risked a glance up to gauge her reaction.

"You don't think I know that?"

"Then why hold anything back? Why not spend every moment living life to the fullest? That way, if it is over, sooner rather than later, you'll have no regrets." He reached out and took her hand, pressing his lips to her fingertips. "If we're going to do this, even if it's just for the summer, I don't want to hold back. I don't want to be careful or keep my feelings to myself. I want everything."

Annie pulled her fingertips from his and picked up her chopsticks. He watched her as she continued to eat, a thoughtful look on her face. He knew she was reconsidering her terms, but he didn't hold out much hope that she'd change her mind. Annie could be irrationally stubborn.

Finally, when she'd finished the carton of sesame chicken, she stood. "I'll think about what you said, but I can't promise anything." With that, she reached for the tie around her waist and undid it. A moment later, her robe lay on the floor around her feet. "You can come to bed with me if you want. If not, I'll understand."

She turned and walked out of the bathroom, leaving him with the cold bath and the remains of dinner. Groaning softly, Gabe leaned back against the edge of the old bathtub. He reached for his wine and downed the rest of the glass in a quick gulp. Why was he pushing so hard? Why not just accept things on her terms?

He poured himself another glass of wine, emptying the bottle. As he stared into the flickering candlelight, he knew letting her go would be impossible.

Bracing his hand on the edge of the tub, he got to his feet. He found Annie in the bedroom, curled up on the bed beneath the thin cotton sheet. Her back was to him, but he could tell by her breathing that she wasn't asleep. He unzipped his flight suit and stripped out of it, kicking off his boots and socks in the process. When he was naked, he pulled back the sheet and crawled into bed with her.

The bed sank under his weight. Gabe reached out and slipped his hand around her waist, then pulled her body back against his, nestling her backside into his lap. They fit perfectly as he always knew they would.

Annie pushed up on her elbow and looked back over her shoulder.

"We're just going to sleep," he said. "Can we try that?"

She smiled and nodded. "Sweet dreams."

ANNIE KNEW HE was still awake. She could tell by the rhythm of his breathing. But when she rolled over to face him, his eyes were closed. This was ridiculous. Here they were, two naked consenting adults and she was just supposed to sleep? Where did this fit in with his big "carpe diem" speech? Seize the day? She was about to seize a whole lot more than that.

Reaching out, she smoothed her fingertips over his brow, then traced the line of his jaw from cheek to chin. He didn't flinch and Annie smiled. If he continued this game, it could be fun, she mused.

She leaned closer and brushed her lips against his. When he still didn't react, she used her tongue, slipping the tip between his lips, teasing him until he moaned softly and opened his eyes.

"You're playing a dangerous game," he warned.

"Then play it with me," Annie said with a laugh. She pushed him back into the bed and crawled on top of him, her legs straddling his hips. "I don't want to play alone."

Though the sheet was between them, she could feel his already hard shaft pressing against the growing damp between her legs. It had been so long since a man had been inside her, the need was almost an ache. Annie began to move against him, rocking her hips until they both felt a tantalizing friction.

"You can go back to sleep," she taunted. "I don't think I'll need more than this to satisfy me."

A low growl rumbled in his throat, and he grabbed her waist and rolled her beneath him so quickly that it took her breath away. He held her wrists above her head as his lips trailed down to her breasts. She twisted, trying to free her hands, but his grip was strong and his intentions clear. He had claimed her body and he was in charge.

Annie closed her eyes as his tongue began to caress her nipple, bringing it to a taut peak in just moments. He nuzzled his face into her flesh as he moved to the other nipple, treating it with the same single-minded care.

When he'd finally had enough, Gabe moved lower, dropping a line of kisses across her belly and stopping when he reached the spot between her legs. Annie knew what was coming and she held her breath, waiting, wondering how she'd react. When his tongue found the center of her desire, she gasped. Wild sensations raced through her body, each nerve tingling until she could barely feel her limbs.

Every thought was focused on that spot as he

flicked his tongue and sucked gently. Her hands were free, but all she could do was clutch at the sheets, as if she were caught on some out-of-control ride and could do nothing but hang on for dear life. He brought her close. Once and then again. But at the very moment that she felt herself tumbling over the edge, he'd suddenly stop, and she'd be left dangling, her body trembling.

Annie whispered her need, begging him for more. But was she speaking out loud or were her words part of the delirium she was experiencing? She writhed beneath his touch, grasping at his hands and drawing his lips closer. And when she was finally certain that there was nothing more she could bear, Gabe finally relented.

In one smooth movement, he drew up along her body and settled his hips between her legs. And then, in the next heartbeat, he was inside her. Annie gasped as he buried himself deep.

"Yes," she whispered. "Please. Yes."

She knew she wasn't making sense, but she couldn't seem to put words together in a logical sentence, and if she could, she wouldn't know what to say. Was this the way it was between two strangers? Two people interested in nothing but physical release? Was that why every sensation seemed multiplied in intensity? Annie had never experienced anything quite as wonderful or frightening as this.

When he began to move, she realized there would be more. The need was still there buried deep inside her, ready to consume her like an ember just waiting for a gust of wind. With each stroke, she felt the heat increase, pulsing, driving her closer and closer to the edge. There was nothing to do to stop it now. The fall was imminent and inevitable.

Gabe whispered soft words of encouragement, and though she didn't want it to end, she had no choice. The ember burst into flame, and her body was consumed by her release. Shudders and spasms took control and she cried out with each one. Every ounce of energy drained from her limbs as the orgasm faded.

And then he followed her, burying himself with one last thrust. Annie held on to him, his face buried in the curve of her neck. For a long time, neither one of them moved. And then Gabe pushed up on his elbows and looked down into her eyes.

Annie smiled at him. "If you're worried about the condom, it's all right."

"You have that covered?"

Annie nodded.

"You knew this was going to happen?"

She nodded again. "I was going to make it happen."

"With me?"

"You were at the top of my list."

He grabbed her waist as he rolled off her, stretching out beside her and dragging her body against his. "After that performance, I should be the only one on your list, don't you think?"

Annie pressed a kiss to the center of his chest, nuzzling her face into the soft line of hair that ran from his collarbone to his belly. "You're kind of full of yourself, aren't you?"

Gabe chuckled, rolling onto his back and throwing his arm over his eyes. "I rocked your world. But feel free to call in the reserves. I think it might be a few days before I'm fit for duty again."

Annie smoothed her hand across his belly until her fingers closed around him. "Maybe I can do something about that."

Gabe sat up and grabbed her wrist, then gently dragged her out of the bed. His body was covered with a thin sheen of perspiration, and it was only then that Annie noticed her hair falling in damp tendrils around her face.

He took her hand and led her back to the bathroom, then helped her into the tub. The water was cool as it rushed over her body, and Annie leaned back and closed her eyes. She smiled when he decided to join her, settling himself in the opposite end.

"I can't remember the last time I took a bath," he said.

"You may want to take a shower before you go back on duty," Annie said. "You're going to smell like a girl."

"I'm going to smell like you," Gabe said. "That's not so bad."

It suddenly occurred to Annie that Gabe might have to work the following day. "What are you doing here? It's a Wednesday night. You usually come on Friday."

"I wanted to see you, and I didn't want to wait."

Annie smiled. "Seize the day," she said, "even if it is a Wednesday." She stretched out her leg on the edge of the tub, and Gabe grabbed it and began to slowly massage her foot.

"I ran into Nellie today," Gabe said. "You know he took a consulting job with Lockheed and we're working on a project together. It's kind of weird to see him out of uniform."

"There is life after the military," Annie said. It might be unreasonable for her to want a man who wasn't living in a war zone half the days of their marriage. But that was her choice. And Gabe would make the choices that were best for him, even if that included a career in the Marines.

"You knew Erik was planning a career in the military when you married him," Gabe said. He reached for her other foot and placed it on his chest. "You knew there was risk."

"I was twenty-one when I married him. I was young and foolish and I didn't really think it through. The military seemed like a glamorous life, especially as the wife of a pilot. I'd seen *Top Gun*. And I was impressed by the uniform."

"So if you had to do it all over again, would you have married him?"

He fixed his gaze on her face, waiting for an answer to his question. But Annie was afraid to say what was in her heart. She'd been in love with Erik and determined to spend the rest of her life with him. He'd swept her off her feet, and when he proposed, she hadn't even thought twice before accepting. To tell the truth, or what she felt was the truth now, would sound like a feeble rationalization. An excuse for her feelings for Gabe.

"Would you?" Gabe repeated. "Tell me the truth, Annie. You can say it to me."

She drew a deep breath, ready to speak, but she couldn't find the right words, words that wouldn't sound selfish and immature. "I loved him. And now he's gone." She braced her hands on the sides of the tub and stood, then grabbed a towel from the rack and wrapped it around her body.

Annie stepped out of the tub and crossed the bathroom to stand in front of the mirror. She stared at her reflection for a long time, yet she barely recognized herself. Who was this woman with the bright spots of color in her cheeks and the flashing green eyes? She may not have a name, Annie mused, but she certainly knew what she wanted.

"I'm not being selfish," she said, "I'm just being practical and honest. I don't want the man I love to die before we've had a chance to live our lives."

"Not every job in the military is on the front lines," Gabe said.

"That sounds nice, but you and I know the truth. You're a pilot, Erik was a pilot. There's always a chance you could get called up, no matter what you were doing."

Annie turned and faced him. She could see the truth in his eyes. He sighed, then tipped his head back to rest on the edge of the tub. "There's nothing wrong with us wanting different lives," she said. "Not everyone is meant to fall in love and live happily-ever-after."

She walked over to the bathtub and held out her hand. "Come on. Let's go back to bed."

"You go," Gabe said. "I think I'm going to drive back to Pax River tonight. I've got some things I need to do early in the morning, and I know I'm not going to get any sleep here."

She sat on the edge of the tub, watching as his fingers twisted through hers, not knowing where her hand began and his ended. He would be so easy to love. And maybe she was in love with him already. But there were just some things that couldn't be negotiated, and a broken heart was one of them.

"If you stay, I promise I'll let you sleep."

"I know you would," Gabe said. "But I'm still going to go. I have a lot to think about. The ride back will give me time." He reached up and cupped her cheek with his hand, then drew her down into a soft kiss. "I'll be back Friday. We need to start working on the boat if you're still planning to leave at the end of August."

Annie hadn't thought about her trip recently. Gabe was right, there was a lot of work to be done. She'd made a promise to herself, and she planned to keep it. She was going to start living her own life with her own adventures. And if that didn't make her happy, she wasn't sure what would.

5

"WHAT THE HELL is this?" Gabe stared down into the tattered cardboard box, picking through the tangle of wires and electronic components that were supposed to be the satellite navigation system for the *Honeymoon*. Zach and Jeremy stood on either side of him.

The two boys had been banned from the water for the weekend, so Gabe had decided to commandeer the pair to help with the *Honeymoon*.

"Whoa," Jeremy said. "That looks seriously vintage."

"I think my grandpa had one of these when he was young," Zach said. "Back in the olden days."

The two boys looked at each other and laughed, then executed a high five. Gabe pointed to the other boxes they'd retrieved from the sail loft. "Open those other boxes," he said.

The boys did as they were told, pulling ancient navigation and radio electronics from each box. Gabe stood back and shook his head. When Annie had told him that she'd already purchased electronics for the boat, he'd expected a stack of brand-new boxes filled with shiny equipment and owner's manuals. Instead, he found rummage-sale junk.

"She isn't really going to put this stuff on her boat, is she?" Zach asked.

"I wouldn't trust this stuff to get me across the bay," Jeremy said.

The trio heard footsteps on the stairs, and they turned to watch as Annie appeared, another box in her hand. When she saw Zach and Jeremy, she frowned. "What are you two guys doing up here?"

"As part of their penance for the catamaran incident, I had them sweep up the sail loft," Gabe said.

Annie looked around her and nodded. "You guys did a nice job."

"You're not really thinking of putting that stuff on your boat, are you?" Zach asked. "I mean, it's a pile of junk."

"Guys, you can check in with me later. Why don't you join your friends and do some sailing? I'm commuting your sentence. Tomorrow is your last day."

The pair didn't need to be asked twice. They grabbed their stuff and headed out, leaving Gabe and Annie to themselves. Annie glanced around at the equipment. "Did you find everything?"

Gabe cursed beneath his breath. "This was all I found. And if this is all you have, then I'm not going to let you get on that boat, much less let you sail it on open water."

"I know it's used equipment," Annie said, a defensive edge to her voice. "But it all works. And you know I can't afford to buy new equipment."

Gabe began to pace the floor. How could he put this without making her angry? He knew what the trip meant to her, and he also knew how short she was on cash. But this was a serious safety issue, especially for someone who planned to sail single-handedly through the Caribbean and up the Pacific Coast.

"You've got the basics here, but that's it. I don't see a radar unit or a satellite phone. Considering you plan to keep to the shoreline, I think you should have both, for your own safety."

Annie sat down on the floor and crossed her legs in front of her. She picked up one of the boxes. "I'm an experienced sailor. I can get along with just a sextant and a compass."

"Don't think you're fucking Christopher Columbus. He had a whole crew with him. You're going to be all alone. What if something breaks?"

"Then I'll deal with it." She looked up at him, then shook her head. "My grandfather taught me to sail with no electronics. He said that no matter what you choose to install, there's always a chance that it will break, and usually it will happen in the worst of circumstances. Just because it's used, doesn't mean that it isn't functional. And just because it's brand-new, doesn't mean that it is. If it doesn't work on the shakedown cruise, then I'll either fix it or replace it."

Gabe reached into the back pocket of his jeans and pulled out a list of priority and recommended items, holding it out to her. "You don't have safety gear yet."

"I can pull that from some of our boats here," Annie explained. "I have it all planned out. Trust me. Lots of people go cruising on a budget." She shoved the list back at him. "If this is going to be a problem for you, I don't need your help. You can find something else to do."

Annie started to rearrange the boxes in front of her. Gabe watched her, noting her frustration when she couldn't find any of the tech manuals. "I thought you said you knew how to install this stuff."

She glared up at him. "I may need the directions." Scrambling to her feet, she brushed the dust off her hands. "I can get them off the internet."

Gabe grabbed her hand as she walked past and pulled her into his embrace. "You need to come with me," he said. He dragged her along behind him, hurrying down the stairs and out into the bright sunshine. His car was parked next to the house, and he opened the passenger door.

"Where are we going?"

"I'll tell you when we get there," Gabe said.

"If you don't tell me now, I'm going to consider this kidnapping."

Gabe gently pushed her into the car and closed the door, then ran around to the driver's side and slipped in behind the wheel. Minutes later they were on the main road, headed north toward Annapolis. Gabe knew there was a good-size marina at Calvert Beach, and he'd seen signs for a marine services business. Knowing Annie's stubborn pride, he was going to have to show her what she needed.

They sped along the highway, the windows of the SUV open to the warm afternoon breeze. It felt good to get away from the sailing school, even if it was for just an hour or two. Annie didn't say much during the trip. Occasionally, she pointed out local landmarks.

When they pulled into the parking lot of the yacht store, Annie didn't seem angry. Instead, she groaned softly. "I can't go in there," she said. "They won't sell me anything anyway."

"Why not?"

"Because I have an outstanding account with them and they want to get paid. No payment, no more credit."

"Well, we'll just have to take care of that."

"No," Annie said. "I'm not going to let you do that. I don't need your help. After this next session, I'll have enough to pay the bill here, and we'll be straight."

He turned to face her. "Listen, Annie, we're not going to come to an agreement about this. If you're determined to make this trip, then I'm just as determined to see that you have what I need to make myself feel better about your safety. So humor me, will you? Here's the deal. I'll pay for what you need, and at the end of the trip, if you sell the boat, you can pay me back then. And if you keep it, we'll work something out."

She considered his suggestion for a long moment, then finally nodded. "All right. But we're going to keep careful account of every penny you spend."

Gabe let out a tightly held breath, happy to finally

get his way. Though he wasn't a fan of her plan to sail to San Diego, he knew that choice had to be hers. If she backed out, the money he spent was a small investment in their future together.

"Then let's go shopping," he said.

When they got inside, he gave Annie the list and told her to buy everything that was marked "priority." After that, they'd discuss the remainder of the items that were "recommended." While she shopped, he found the manager and made arrangements to pay her past-due account along with any future credit she may require.

Although Gabe knew she'd object, he felt a certain satisfaction in being able to take care of her. Until now, he'd eased her physical desires and soothed her emotional crises, but that seemed like simple human nature. This was real and tangible.

He decided to leave Annie to her shopping, knowing that if he was at her side, they'd probably argue about her choices. He'd be happy with whatever she decided, as long as it was brand-new.

He found a small gathering of chairs near the service area and grabbed a free cup of coffee from a pot that was warming. A selection of sailing and boating magazines were spread out on the table, and he picked one up and began to page through it. An article caught his eye, a firsthand account of a sailing trip around Australia, and he settled in to read it.

Gabe hadn't realized how much time had passed, and the next thing he knew, he looked up to find Annie standing nearby with a cart stacked with boxes.

He grinned. "Wow. Good job. I hope you remembered the life raft."

"I did," she said. "It's a good one. It was on sale because it's last year's model, so I saved three hundred dollars."

Gabe patted the seat beside him and she sat down. "That wasn't so hard, was it? Sometimes it's all right to compromise. If anything ever happened to you, I don't know what I would do with myself. And if this will keep you safe, then it's money well spent."

He slipped his arm around her shoulders and pulled her closer, his lips brushing against hers, his tongue tracing the crease of her mouth. Annie sighed softly and melted into him, her hands splayed across his chest.

These random acts of affection had been occurring more and more recently. After their first night together, she'd been careful outside the bedroom to maintain a distance, knowing that the students might notice. But now, away from the school, she was perfectly comfortable with touching him in public. Gabe considered it a major victory.

"I have an idea," Gabe said.

Annie smiled and ran a fingertip across his lower lip. "I have lots of ideas. Would you like to hear some of them? One of them involves sailing naked across the Chesapeake. Are you interested?"

Gabe kissed her again, this time lingering over her lips. "When would we do this?"

"The week after next is Fourth of July. We don't have any campers that week. The counselors stay and catch up on boat maintenance and cabin cleaning. And they have a little fun. If we work at it, we can get most of this stuff installed by then and give it a good test."

"Naked," he said.

She frowned. "Haven't you done that before? Erik told me stories about you two taking a boat out on a weekend leave. I think he said you were in Greece."

Gabe knew the weekend she was talking about. Only, he wasn't Erik's sailing partner. He remembered a pretty blonde college student from Sweden. "Oh, yeah, I remember that now. You get enough beers in Erik and he was always taking his clothes off."

Annie smiled wistfully. "Yeah, that was one of his things. We always had to talk before we went to a party, and I had to threaten him that if he didn't keep his clothes on, he'd be sleeping on the sofa."

"If we want to be ready by then, I'm going to have to drive back and forth from Pax River every day so we can work on the boat in the evenings."

Over the past few weeks, Gabe had learned a few things about women. And, in particular, Annie Foster Jennings. She was determined to make her own decisions, so there was no use fighting with her once a decision had been made. If he didn't want her to go, then he would just have to find a more tempting reason for her to stay.

Gabe wasn't sure what that might be, but for now he was going to get her ready to sail for the Panama Canal at the end of August. "I bet Nellie would like to come back and forth with me," Gabe said. "He could help with the boat and get some time away from the base."

"We could invite Lisa and the kids to come up for a visit. I'm going to call her when I get home."

Considering that Lisa was Gabe's fiercest advocate, he was satisfied that everything was moving in the right direction. And a few days of naked sailing on the Chesapeake was something to look forward to.

"I'M NOT SURE this was a good idea."

Annie slipped her leg across Gabe's thighs and rested her chin on his naked chest. The sun was just beginning to brighten the east-facing windows of her bedroom and the morning birds were singing as they waited for the light of day.

By her reckoning, it was only a matter of an hour or two before Gabe would have to leave for the base. She twisted around to look at the bedside clock, confirming her guess. They had another ninety minutes before he had to leave.

Gabe frowned as he smoothed his hand through her hair. "What? Sleeping with me every night isn't a good idea?"

"We don't get a whole lot of sleep," she said. "And I'm falling behind on all the work I have to do for the sailing school. Thank God I have a good crew of counselors this year."

"We have to get the boat done. You can't do that yourself, but with Nellie and me working on it, we should have it ready in a few days."

Nellie had taken up residence on the screened-in porch, preferring to spend his nights with cool breezes and the comfort of an old hammock. Unlike Gabe, he always seemed well rested in the morning.

"What if you have to fly today? You're going to be tired, and your reflexes are going to be slow."

"If I need to fly, I'll put it off until tomorrow," Gabe said. "Besides, the work I'm doing doesn't really require my flying skills. Mostly my technical expertise."

"What are you doing?" Annie asked.

"I can't tell you. It's classified."

Annie pushed up to sit beside him. "Really? Like CIA classified?"

"No, more like Department of Defense classified. I wrote a report a few years ago pointing out some problems we were having with a particular system on our aircraft. They wanted me to work on this new project and had to give me security clearance in order to even look at it."

"At least it gets you out of harm's way," Annie said.

"It's not what I do best. I'm a good pilot, Annie. Hell, I'm a great pilot, and I'd rather be doing the job I was trained for."

She stared at him for a long moment, her expression cool, her eyes narrowed in anger. Was it that hard to understand how she felt? Any job that involved risking his life just wasn't worth it, at least not in her mind. "Yeah? That's what Erik always said and look at where it got him."

She crawled out of bed and grabbed her robe, then

wrapped it tightly around her naked body. So she was cranky this morning. The lack of sleep was starting to get to her, as well. Annie grabbed her brush from the dresser and dragged it through her tangled hair.

"I'm sorry," she murmured. "I shouldn't have said that." In truth, it shouldn't make any difference to her what he did for a living. Their agreement had involved a physical relationship only, with no strings attached.

But from the moment they began, her feelings had been changing. It was impossible for her to look at Gabe and see just the physical pleasures he offered her. He was more than just a sexy body who satisfied her in the bedroom. He was a man of incredible inner conviction and quiet strength, a man who took care of the people in his life without any thought to his own needs. He could be stubborn and opinionated, but then, so was she.

Was she falling in love with him? Annie had promised herself that she wouldn't let that happen. But Gabe wasn't making it easy on her. He was quite clear about how he felt, and though he hadn't professed his fondness recently, she could see it in everything he did for her.

"I'm sorry," she said. "I'm not being fair. I expect you to allow me to live my life by my choices, and I'm not willing to make the same concessions for you."

He held out his hand and she returned to him, crawling back into bed beside him. Gabe settled her in the curve of his arm. "Let me ask you something, and I want you to be completely honest. If I were a plumber or an accountant, would that change how you felt about me?"

Annie considered the question, then shook her head. "You'd never want to be a plumber or an accountant. You'd be miserable. You're a pilot. That's who you are."

"And you can't fall in love with me because I am a pilot," he said.

"Yes," Annie replied.

"So, the way I see it, there's no way I'm going to get the girl in the end." He pulled the pillow over his face. "Nice guys always finish last."

"I'm not the only single woman in the world," she said.

He pulled the pillow aside. "You're the only single woman I want to be with."

Annie crawled out of bed. "I'm going to go put some coffee on. At least I can make you a decent breakfast before you leave. Maybe that will give you the energy to make it through the day."

To Annie's surprise, Nellie was sitting at the kitchen table when she got down to the kitchen. He had fixed himself some eggs and toast, and was sipping freshly made coffee. "You're up early," she said.

"Mmm-hmm," he said, his mouth full of toast. "I'm always up at this time. For me, 5:00 a.m. is normal. Breeze is always up with the sun."

"Did you sleep well?" Annie asked.

Nellie laughed. "Are you kidding? At home, I share a bed with my wife, my dog and my two youngest kids. Here, I have a hammock all to myself. What do you think?"

Annie grabbed a mug of coffee and sat across from him. "I'm so happy for you and Lisa."

He shrugged. "Yeah, I suppose. I'm not getting RPGs launched at me every other day. That's a plus."

"Do you miss it?" Annie asked.

"Yeah," Nellie said. "Of course I do. I got to fly almost every day, in some of the fastest jets made. I was protecting my country, our soldiers. And I was helping some people who were just trying to live peacefully in a country that offers them so little hope. I was good at my job. Now I'm just doing a job." He paused. "I've been thinking about applying to the airlines. The pay is great, and I'd get to fly again."

"Does Lisa know?"

Nellie shook his head. "No. I don't think she'll be happy. I was going to apply first and then tell her if I made it in. You know, Angel has this right. He's single, he makes his own decisions. Hell, I would have loved to go to test pilot's school, but Lisa would have flipped."

"Gabe is going to test pilot's school?" Annie asked.

"Yeah, he starts in February. Right after he finishes up this project. Didn't he tell you?"

"No," she said. "But then, I'm not going to be around. I'll be on my trip by September. That's probably why he didn't say anything."

"Yeah, that's probably it. It's good for him. Opens up lots of career possibilities."

"He mentioned he wanted to be an astronaut," Annie said.

"He's hella smart, Angel is," Nellie said. "I'd put money on him any day. Once he puts his mind to something, there's no stopping him."

"Yeah," Annie said, forcing a smile. "I know how that is."

Nellie pushed back from the table and picked up his dishes, then carried them to the sink. "Can I make you some breakfast? I'm great with eggs but even better with pancakes. I can make them look like all sorts of animals."

"I'm fine," Annie said. "And leave your dishes. I'll take care of them."

He grabbed his mug and filled it again. "I'm going to go finish wiring the radar unit on your boat. Tell Angel I want to leave a little earlier. Oh, and I talked to Lisa last night, and she said she'd be here early afternoon on Friday."

"I'm looking forward to her visit," she said.

"Now we just need to find you a man and we'll all be happy," Nellie teased, then walked out into the early-morning light.

Annie sighed softly. She had a perfectly wonderful man, right upstairs in her bed. The only problem was his affection for his very dangerous job. Jeez, she'd seen *The Right Stuff*. Gabe was going to go from chopper pilot to test pilot to space shuttle pilot? It just got worse and worse.

If she allowed herself to love Gabe, then she'd never sleep through the night again. Her sailing trip was exactly what she needed. To get over Erik. And to get over Gabe. After she got back from San Diego, she'd find a nice, normal, earthbound man who came home every night for dinner and always drove the speed limit.

Then she could live happily-ever-after.

"WHY DID WE have to leave early?" Gabe asked. "We're not due back on base until ten."

"I needed to talk to you, and I wanted to make sure we had enough time."

"It's an hour drive to Pax River," Gabe said. "What do we have to—" He paused. "We're not going to talk about Annie. I told you, she's made her decision about me. As long as I'm flying, she's not interested in a relationship. And considering what happened to her first husband, I really can't blame her. End of discussion."

"Well, this is only about Annie. It has nothing to do with you. That is, until you get involved."

Gabe glanced over at Nellie, slumped down in the passenger seat, dressed in a shirt and tie, his gaze hidden by dark sunglasses. "All right. Go ahead."

"I mentioned to her that you were going to test pilot's school in February. She didn't seem to know about that. Sorry. I thought you would have said something."

"No, it's all right," Gabe said. "I thought I had mentioned it to her. It doesn't make much difference. She's going to be sailing to California by then."

"That's what she said," Nellie replied.

"So, that's it?"

"No," Nellie said. "No, that's not it. I talked to Lisa last night, and she told me that she had a call from Darlene Lewis. She's Major Ted Lewis's much younger second wife. He's the commander of the airfield at Miramar."

"Oh, hell, I know where this is going. I heard the rumors about Breaker and Darlene. He told me there was nothing going on."

"They weren't rumors," Nellie said. "She and Erik spent a lot of time in the sack."

Gabe felt a wave of anger surge inside of him. Sure, he and Breaker had stopped talking about his conquests. And Gabe had chosen to believe he'd stopped. But now that he had proof his best friend had continued to cheat on the woman they both loved, it didn't sit well.

He felt the betrayal as deeply as Annie might. Their marriage had never been a true meeting of hearts and souls. It had been nothing more than a mirage, a perfect image that dissolved in the light of day.

"Turns out, Darlene was so pleased with his performance that she gave him a very expensive watch, a Rolex, that she took from her husband's rather impressive collection. And now she needs it back. She called Lisa because she thought she might be willing to ask Annie for it. If Annie ever had it in the first place."

"You're kidding me. You're going to break this news to Annie over a damn watch? Tell me how much the thing costs and we'll just buy a new one and give it to her."

"Thought of that. Can't be done," Nellie said. "It's a custom watch and it's worth over a quarter million dollars. I don't know about you, but I don't have that kind of cash just lying around."

"Are you sure she has it?" Gabe asked.

"That's where you come in. I'm thinking you can look around and see if you can find it. And if you do, just grab it and we'll give it back to her."

"No way. I'm not getting mixed up in this mess. I've kept enough of Breaker's secrets from her over the years. I won't do it anymore."

"Do you want this woman to go right to Annie? Do you really want Annie to find out that her husband cheated on her? She has her memories of him and what their marriage was. This will turn everything upside down for her. And if she finds out that you knew, well, she's not going to like that either."

"Are you kidding me?" Gabe asked. "Breaker knew how I felt about his screwing around. And he promised me that he'd stopped. I guess I was wrong to trust him."

"Yeah, you were wrong. Hell, there could be others. I just hope he doesn't have some kid out there somewhere who's going to want a share of his death benefits."

Gabe's grip tightened on the steering wheel. "No, there's no kid. At least not that he knew about. He would have told me that. He would have wanted a kid of his to be taken care of, and he would have come to me or you about that."

"I hope you're right," Nellie said.

"I hope so, too." A long silence spun out around them before Gabe spoke again. "All right. I'll look for it. Hell, maybe she hasn't bothered to go through his stuff yet. Maybe she hasn't even seen the damn thing."

They spent the rest of the ride chatting about work issues, but Gabe was only marginally focused on their earlier conversation. Instead, his thoughts were fixed on the situation Nellie had described.

Though he'd always wondered what Annie would think if she knew the truth about her husband's philandering, he didn't want to see her hurt, especially not now. She was rebuilding her life without Erik, and she'd finally made the decision to move on.

If she learned of even a tiny part of his womanizing, she'd never be able to trust again. And his chances of winning her heart would be close to impossible. Was he selfish? Or was he just determined to protect her? Gabe wasn't really sure, but his instincts told him to keep quiet and hope that the storm blew over before Annie even realized that it was raining.

When they got to the base, Gabe headed for the barracks to grab a quick shower and change into his flight suit. But when he got there, he found a message taped to his door. "Meet with Captain Jack Scanlon, 10:00, River's Edge Conference Center, room 112."

The note had come from his commanding officer here on the base, without an explanation. Scanlon wasn't a name he recognized. He hadn't served with him, and he wasn't in his chain of command either here or in Afghanistan.

Gabe couldn't help but wonder if maybe someone had noticed his late-morning arrivals and early-afternoon departures. He'd been told that the hours for his duty at Pax River were flexible, but in all honesty, he had been taking advantage.

Not knowing what the meeting was about, he decided to change into his service uniform. He hurried through his shower and shave and was at the door of the conference center at exactly 10:00 a.m.

He found the room and rapped on the door, then stepped inside at the order of "Enter." Scanlon crossed the room and held out his hand. "Captain Pennington. Thanks so much for agreeing to meet with me on such short notice."

"No problem," Gabe said, glancing around the room. "I'm not sure what this is about."

Scanlon pointed to a chair across from the sofa. "Sit down. Would you like something to drink? I've got coffee here, but we could get you something cold if you prefer."

"I'm fine. Maybe we could just get down to business," he said.

Scanlon nodded. "Well, then, let me explain. I'm the deputy superintendent at the naval academy. I've been tasked with coordinating a new recruiting plan for instructors and your name came up. I'm here to find out if you might want to consider a job on our teaching staff."

Gabe swallowed a gasp. "Me?"

"We've had our eye on you for a while. You graduated second in your class, you had some of the highest marks in your squadron at flight school. You've nearly completed your master's degree in electrical engineering online while serving in a war zone. That's quite a list of achievements."

"Thank you."

"Now you've been accepted into test pilot's school with the aim of giving NASA a try. We'd rather you consider working for us."

"Teach," he said, unable to believe what he was hearing. Gabe had always had an affection for the academy. "I've never thought about that career path."

"You'd begin as an instructor. We'd want you to get a PhD, and then you'd advance from there."

"I don't know. I guess I'd like to think about it. I'm a pilot. I can see teaching at flight school, but this is a bit different."

"Well, we'd like you to consider it. We're going to have some staff openings over these next couple years, and we'd like to find a few good Marines to join us. And we'd like to invite you up to Annapolis to meet with the superintendent, Vice Admiral Conroy. We can have you sit in with some of the instructors, and you'll get a chance to see how they work."

"I'd like that," Gabe said.

"Are you married? Engaged?"

"Does that make a difference?"

"No. Only that teaching at the academy would give you a pretty normal lifestyle for the military. Sometimes, that's an attraction. Home for dinner with the wife and the kids every night. A house in the suburbs, good schools, weekends free. I know my wife likes it."

"I can appreciate that," Gabe said.

Scanlon stood. "Well, if you have any other questions or would like to come for a visit, just give me a call."

"Thank you."

"Thank you, Captain Pennington. And I hope to hear from you soon."

Gabe walked out of the meeting room and headed back to his car. But then he turned and headed in the opposite direction, to the river. He found a seat and stretched his legs out in front of him.

He thought back to that kiss that he'd shared with Annie in the boat shed in San Diego. Since that moment, his life had shifted. He'd been just an ordinary pilot, an ace behind the controls of a SuperCobra. Now he was a pilot with options.

His cell phone buzzed, and Gabe pulled it out of his pocket. He switched it on. "Yeah, Nellie. I'm on my way. I had a quick meeting I had to take care of."

"The engineers installed the system in a Venom, and they want you to take it on a test flight. That's scheduled for noon. Are you okay with that?"

"Yeah, sure," Gabe said. "I'm fine."

"All right. I need you to check it out before you take it up. Get over here."

"I just have to stop at the barracks and change into my flight suit."

He switched off his phone, then levered to his feet. He'd have to consider all his options later. And after he'd considered them all, then he'd have to decide how Annie might react to a major change in his lifestyle.

Afghanistan seemed like another life. He'd been back for two months, and he felt himself losing his edge. The adrenaline was like a drug, an addiction that had to be fed or it lost its power. Maybe it was time, Gabe mused. Maybe his odds had run out and the universe was telling him he'd already flown his last combat mission.

He'd always told himself that he'd trust his instincts, and he'd know if and when he should get out. But it seemed like the decision wasn't up to him. The fates had other plans, and some of those plans included Annie.

He glanced down at his phone, his finger hovering over the speed dial for Annie. He wanted to tell her his news, to find out what she thought. But it would be better to tell her in person. He'd be able to gauge her true feelings if he could look into her eyes.

She could change her mind. She could decide to let her heart rule her head and let herself fall in love again. Maybe he was hoping for too much, but what the hell. If he didn't believe, then it might never happen.

6

ANNIE STARED ACROSS the table at Gabe, sipping at her wine as she listened to him tell a funny story about his first time in a helicopter. It involved six corn dogs and a county fair and an eight-year-old who'd saved his birthday and Christmas money to buy the ride.

Nellie and Lisa sat on the other side of the table, the remains of a steak dinner spread out on the checkered tablecloth. They'd finished two bottles of wine and were halfway through the third when Lisa stood, holding her glass of water out to the others.

"I'd like to make a toast," she said, swinging her arm around until her water dumped out on Gabe's lap. "Yes, it's water, but hey, I'm pregnant."

Annie, Gabe and Nellie held up their glasses and cheered. "To water," Gabe said.

"To babies," Annie added.

"And to my beautiful wife, who is blooming like the rose she has always been," Nellie finished. "I love you, darlin'."

"All right, all right," Gabe said, picking up the bottle of sparkling water. He graciously refilled her glass. "Carry on."

"To my friend Annie and her friend Gabe. May the two of you discover that love is all you need." She began to sing the refrain from the Beatles song as she danced around over to Annie and wrapped her arms around her neck.

"I think it's time for Lisa to go to bed," Nellie said. "We've got a busy day tomorrow, and we don't want Mommy to have the flu while we're touring the Air and Space Museum."

"Are you sure you don't want to come along with us?" Lisa asked.

Annie gave her a kiss on the cheek. "We need to work on the boat tomorrow. I have Gabe for a whole day. I need to make good use of him."

Lisa giggled. "Oh, I can think of much better things to do with him than making him work on that boat."

"Take her to bed," Gabe ordered.

Nellie got up from the table and scooped his wife into his arms. "Come on, darlin'. We've got a bed full of children waiting for us."

"Don't forget the dog. Oh, you don't mind watching him tomorrow? He's really good. He hardly ever poops in the house. I'm talking about the dog, not Nellie."

"No problem," Annie said with a laugh.

They listened as Nellie stumbled up the stairs. Gabe got out of his chair and circled the table. He turned her chair around, then pulled her to her feet, dragging her into his arms. "Hello," he murmured.

"Hi," Annie said.

"I've missed you."

"I've been here all night long."

"You know what I mean," Gabe said. "I'm used to touching you whenever I want to."

"I know. It's a little strange with Nellie and Lisa. I don't want them to think we're a couple."

"No, we wouldn't want them to think that. So, what exactly are we? We can't be lovers because we don't love each other."

"I don't think the term *lovers* really excludes people who aren't in love. But I think friends with benefits is probably a better way to think of us. We are friends and we do enjoy some extra benefits."

"You wouldn't happen to have a list of those benefits, would you? Just so we can be clear."

Annie wriggled in his embrace, pressing her hips against his. "I don't have a written list, but I could show you." She grabbed his hand and led him to the back door.

"Where are we going?"

"It's a little crowded in the house," she said. "I've got a place we can go." He followed her out into the darkness, and Annie led him to the water. The *Honeymoon* sat at anchor, just off the shore, the mast gleaming in the moonlight.

"You want to go out there?"

Annie nodded. "It's private. No one will hear us.

We can get naked and look at the stars." She started to unbutton her dress, and Gabe reached out to stop her.

"We're not going to swim out there. I'll go get the dinghy."

"No, it's not that far," Annie insisted.

"Sweetheart, that water is cold. And there are parts of me that have been hot for you since the moment I got home. And when those two things collide, it's not going to be a pretty sight."

Annie felt a warm blush rise on her cheeks. "Oh. Sorry. I didn't think of that." She waved her hand. "We'll take the dinghy."

They found it resting on the shore a few yards away. Gabe flipped it upright and grabbed the oars, then pushed it out into the calm water of the bay. Gabe had found the little fiberglass boat in one of the sheds and cleaned it up, then christened it *Honey Bee*. He'd painted the name on the stern with a little illustration of a bee before presenting it to her the previous weekend.

Annie dragged her hand through the water as they glided out to the *Honeymoon*. The soft splash of the oars in the water slowed as they approached, and she reached out to catch the gunwale on the boat before standing up and tying the dinghy to a cleat.

She crawled onto the deck, then jumped down into the cockpit, turning around to look at the moon as it dipped close to the horizon. She'd learned to sail from her grandfather when she was just five, and Annie sometimes felt more comfortable on a sailboat than she did on dry land.

"My grandfather used to ferry boats from the East Coast down to the Caribbean every summer. At least two or three trips. He used to take me along with him, just the two of us, and we'd motor down the Intercoastal Waterway. Almost a thousand miles from the Chesapeake to just north of Miami." She reached out and ran her hand along the boom, then ducked under it and sat on the opposite side of the cockpit. "We'd do about fifty or sixty miles a day, just motoring along. And when we got to Miami, we'd step the mast and sail into blue water. I learned everything from him."

"Is he still alive?" Gabe asked.

Annie nodded. "He lives down in Key West. He runs a boat refurbishing business. He's eighty-four and still goes out sailing almost every day. I'm going to visit him when I do my trip."

Gabe threw his arms over the boom and watched her from the other side, the moon casting his handsome face in light and shadows. "He sounds like a great guy. I'd love to meet him."

"Oh, he'd like you. He loves talking about the military. He's a real history buff."

"You said he was in the Navy. Did your other grandfather serve?" Gabe asked.

"No, he wanted to. But he's partially blind in one eye. He had an accident when he was a child." She tucked her legs under her. "What about you? Did either of your grandfathers serve?"

"My mom's dad was a bomber pilot during World War II," he said. "We used to go to the airport together and watch the planes come in and out. He was there when I took my first helicopter ride. And he gave me money for flying lessons when I was in high school. He died the year after I graduated from Annapolis."

A long silence grew between them, and Annie listened to the gentle lap of water against the hull of the sailboat. In just a few months, this boat would be her home. She'd probably sit in this very spot on a starry night. And remember being here with him. It wouldn't just be the conversation she'd remember. Tonight, they'd share much more.

"Sometimes I feel like I barely know you," she murmured. "And then other times, it feels like we've known each other forever. How can that be?"

He bent down beneath the boom and joined her, stretching out on the bench seat, his arm draped across the back. "I don't know," Gabe said. He reached for her hair and took a strand between his fingertips. "How am I going to get along without you?"

Annie laughed. "I'm the one who's going to be all alone."

"I wish you didn't have to be," he said.

"That's the point, though, isn't it? It's like my quest. I'm walking into the wilderness to search for answers."

"What kind of answers do you need? Maybe I can save you some time and give them to you."

Annie reached over and smoothed her palm against his chest. "I need to figure out my future. I expected to spend it with a husband and a family, and now I'm alone. I need a career, a way to pay the bills."

"You know I'm happy to help with that even though I know you don't need my help," Gabe offered.

"Ah, now you're starting to get the idea," she teased. "It sure has taken you enough time."

Gabe laughed. "Yes, it has. But it's not just about money. Whatever you need, I want you to know that I'm here." He bent close and brushed a kiss across her lips. "What do you need, Annie? Tell me."

A smile twitched at the corners of her mouth. "Stand up. And take your shirt off."

Gabe's eyebrow arched, his expression of bemusement very clear in the light reflected off the water. "Really? We're going to go there?"

"Isn't that why we came out here?"

With a reluctant groan, Gabe grabbed the bottom of his T-shirt and dragged it over his head, exposing a chiseled chest that looked like carved marble in the moonlight. "Better?" he asked.

"Not quite." She pointed to his zipper. "Now the pants. And take your shoes off first."

This brought another chuckle. "Bossy, bossy."

Annie sat back and watched as he stripped off the last of his clothes and tossed them aside. He was the most beautiful man she'd ever seen, his body lean and finely muscled, his skin tan and smooth. She clutched her fingers into a fist, resisting the impulse to touch him. Gabe had taught her that the best things in the bedroom were worth waiting for.

"Now turn around, slowly." Usually, Gabe was the one who took control, but for some reason he was letting Annie have the pleasure. When he finally faced her again, his shaft was nearly erect. She reached out and wrapped her fingers around him, gently, drawing him closer.

Her lips found the tip, and she took him into her mouth. He was hot and hard, yet his skin was as soft as silk. Annie took him as deep as she could, then slowly retreated, leaving a damp trail from her tongue and lips. Slowly, she set up a rhythm, her hand wrapped around the base of his shaft and her lips at the tip.

Over their previous nights together, Annie had learned what pleased him. Sometimes rough, sometimes gentle, she carried him toward his release, but then at the last moment drew him away. They edged closer each time. And with his retreat, he grew harder and more desperate.

Gabe furrowed his fingers through her hair, brushing a strand aside so he could watch what she was doing. Annie felt powerful, pleasuring him in this way. But she knew he wouldn't be satisfied unless they finished with him buried deep inside her.

When she knew he couldn't take anymore, she stood and slowly began to remove her clothes. She took her time, teasing him with each piece of skin exposed, smoothing her hands over her body and creating a delicious friction that brought goose bumps in the cool night air.

This was what it would be like every night if they were together. She could imagine the warm nights sailing through the Caribbean, the scent of exotic flowers in the air, songbirds calling from thickets of palm trees and scrub pine.

They'd anchor the boat on a sandbar off some deserted cay. Like children, they'd play in the water, their naked skin burnished dark by the sun. Every day would be an adventure, something new to explore, something important to learn about each other.

As he pulled her into his arms and kissed her, Annie wanted to stop him and say *come with me*. She simply couldn't imagine going a month, much less six, without this passion in her life. Three simple words. An invitation to continue what they'd begun on land. But Annie knew that the meaning of her trip would change the moment he stepped on board.

Was she falling in love with him? She'd been asking herself that very question over and over again and she still hadn't come up with a suitable answer.

She'd been so young the first time that she barely remembered what it felt like. It was so simple back then, just two kids who couldn't keep their hands off each other. But she was a grown woman now with a life of her own and choices to be made. Love was no longer just a simple choice, yes or no, black or white.

As his lips came down on hers and his tongue found hers, Annie pushed her worries aside. There was still time, she thought, as his fingers slipped between her legs. Plenty of time to figure it all out.

EVERY NERVE IN his body was on fire, and Gabe felt as if he were about to burst into flames. Every place she touched was left burning, like a brand on his body.

She'd brought him to an extraordinary state, his shaft hard and aching for release, his body ready to follow.

Now her hand took over the task, fingers wrapped gently around his erection as she stroked in a purposeful rhythm. He watched her, still amazed that all his fantasies had come to life. How many times had he thought about this, then scolded himself for a silent betrayal of his best friend.

Yet he couldn't feel guilty now. In his mind, she'd always been his. They were meant to be together. Destiny had finally taken hold of their lives and brought them together. There were so many things he wanted to say to her, so many promises he wanted to make. But she wasn't ready.

Gabe sat on the bench seat in the cockpit, pulling her down with him. She straddled his thighs, her bent knees pressed up against his hips. Gabe slid lower, until his shaft found the damp spot between her legs. Then, reaching up, he pulled her mouth down to meet his.

Kissing Annie was always an adventure in seduction. It wasn't just a simple meeting of lips and tongues, a prelude to something more tantalizing. Kissing was the way they communicated as they made love, a silent language that conveyed every want and need in very explicit terms.

She moved above him, shifting her body against his erection until he was halfway inside her. Gabe groaned softly. This battle for control always made for a deeper passion between them, but tonight, he didn't want to fight. He was happy to let her make all the moves. He wanted to sit back and enjoy.

Gabe smiled as she began to rock above him, leaning forward with each slow, delicious withdrawal. He felt every different sensation—the faint breeze on his damp skin, the tug of her fingers in his hair and the warmth of her lips on his.

He was completely captivated by this woman, and there was nothing he could do to stop himself. Hell, why would he want to stop himself?

Wrapping his hands around her waist, Gabe slowed her pace, determined to maintain control for as long as possible. But Annie was already swept up in the drive toward her release, taking him along with her. "Slow down," he whispered.

"No," she replied.

Gabe chuckled softly. "That's what I love about you. You know exactly what you want and go after it."

Annie stared down at him, a wicked smile on her face. "And what do I want?" She pushed up on her knees and suddenly he was no longer inside her. "Do I want to torment you?"

"Yes," Gabe said, pulling her back down until he was buried in her warmth. "I think about this all the time. I'll be in the middle of calibrating a sensor and an image of you will flash in my mind. And I'll have to start all over again. You're a dangerous woman."

"And I was just thinking that you were the dangerous one," Annie said.

She rose up above him, leaving his heat exposed to the cool night air. Gabe waited for her to come down again, anticipating the incredible sensation of burying himself deep inside her. He watched her for a long moment, then slipped his hands around her hips and pulled her back down. A moment later, he was inside her again, her backside pressed against his belly.

Gabe reached around to touch her. Many times they took turns reaching their release. But those moments when they came together were powerful and intense. Tonight, she wanted to feel that, the heat and the spasms, the complete surrender of her body to his touch.

And when it finally happened, when she cried out his name and dissolved into shudders of pleasure, Gabe realized how perfect they were together. He'd never experienced this kind of intimacy with any other woman. She'd invaded his soul and captured his heart, controlled his body and muddled his mind, and yet he was willing to give her even more. Whatever he possessed was hers for the asking.

Knees weak, he pulled her down to sit on his lap, her body still open to his touch. "It feels different out here," he said. "It's just us. Completely alone together."

She curled up, snuggling against him. "Just think of the tan you could get. Or no tan lines."

"I can think of other advantages."

"Like what?"

He stood, scooping her up with him. "Like we can go for a swim without having to take the time to undress."

"Oh, no," she said, wriggling in his arms. "No, no, no!"

"You were all ready to swim earlier."

"It was just an excuse to get you naked," she cried.

He set her on her feet, then stepped up to the deck. He maneuvered over the lifelines, then stood, poised to dive into the dark water. "Come on. It'll feel great."

"You jump first," she said. "I know you. You'll push me in and then laugh at me from the deck."

Gabe held out his hand. "No, we jump together. Come on, Annie. Trust me."

Finally, she shook her head and relented. She crawled up beside him, clutching his hand. "It's going to be colder now that we're all hot and sweaty."

"It's going to feel great."

He counted down, and when he shouted "Jump," they both leaped off the side. Annie was right. The water *was* cold, but only at first. As they came back to the surface, still holding hands, he grabbed her around the waist, kicking his legs to keep her afloat.

They played in the water until they were both exhausted and could barely manage another stroke. It was a refreshing end to a long, hot day, and as Gabe helped Annie up the swim ladder on the stern of the boat, he thought about the trip she was planning to take.

She'd be all alone the entire way, vulnerable to the weather and shipping lanes and pirates that prowled the waters off Mexico and Central America. It could prove to be a difficult trip to complete, and just as difficult for the one left behind—him.

Gabe found a blanket in the locker beneath the cockpit seat and wrapped it around her naked body.

Then, pulling her into his arms, he rubbed her back until his blood began to warm again.

"Promise me, if you decide to swim on your trip, you'll tie yourself to the boat. And wear a life jacket."

She glanced over at him. "What? Why?"

"If you're out in the middle of nowhere and the boat drifts away, what are you going to do?"

"Swim over to wherever it drifted."

"What if you get a cramp? Or get stung by a jellyfish? Or surrounded by sharks?"

Annie laughed. "You're kidding, right?"

"I'm not. You're going to need to think about these things. Every action you take has a multitude of consequences, and some of them are very bad and could get you killed."

"I know that. And I'll be careful, I promise."

"And whenever you're on deck or in the cockpit, you need to wear your safety harness. One slip and you could end up in the water, waving at your boat as it sails away without you."

She gave him a playful salute. "Yes, sir. Aye-aye, sir."

Gabe grabbed her hand and pulled it down. "I'm not kidding, Annie. I don't think you realize how hard this is going to be for me. I'm going to be left to imagine all sorts of horrible things. I need to know that you won't take any risks."

"All right." She held up her hand. "I swear that I will always practice the highest safety standards while sailing the *Honeymoon*." She paused. "You're still not satisfied."

"Something could go wrong out there and I'd never know. You could fall off the boat and be floating in open water, and no one would be there to save you."

"You need to stop worrying so much. You're going to have to chill or you'll go crazy."

"Chill. Do you have any idea how I feel about you? I've waited for years to know you, to be able to touch you and kiss you. And when I think about losing you, it gets me just a little crazy."

"And there you have it," Annie said. "Now maybe you can understand how I felt on the day Erik left for another deployment. That hopeless knowledge that no matter how much I cared, how much I prayed, it wouldn't make any difference. Fate will always have its way."

"This is not the same," Gabe said. "You have a choice. To go or not to go. I don't have a choice. It's my job."

"But it's the same feeling," she said. "And where would it stop? I could walk out the door and get hit by a bus. Would you chain me up in the bedroom and never let me venture out in the world again?"

"Honestly? That doesn't sound like such a bad idea," Gabe murmured.

"I'm leaving at the end of August. A lot of things can change between now and then, but my mind isn't one of them. I'm going. That's it. End of discussion."

"And some things will never change," Gabe said.

He couldn't imagine a day when he didn't love her anymore or when he wasn't concerned about her safety. But he knew if he pushed too hard, Annie would resist. She might even just push him out of her life entirely.

Was he wrong? Was he holding on too tightly? Every instinct told him to let her go, to give her the freedom to follow her own dreams. He'd done that once before, and she'd married Erik.

Annie held the blanket open, inviting him into the warmth. Gabe slipped his arms around her waist and picked her up, pressing his lips into the curve of her neck. "You have to let me worry," he said.

"And you have to let me go," Annie countered.

For now, he'd let it go. Though he'd never truly been in love before, he knew a few things from listening to Nellie and other married friends. Sometimes it was better to retreat and take up the battle at another time.

He had two more months left to make her fall so madly in love with him that she wouldn't want to leave. Two months to convince her that loving a Marine pilot wasn't the end of the world. Two months to decide what changes he was willing to make in his own life to compromise with her dreams.

Two more months to finally realize that this wasn't about his own selfish needs. It was about Annie and what she wanted out of life. It might take more strength than he possessed, but there was no other way. From now on, he wouldn't fight her. He'd encourage her.

"Look at those stars," Annie said. "Can you imagine what it used to be like, hundreds of years ago, when all a sailor had was the stars to help him navigate? Columbus discovered America."

"I wouldn't give a whole lot of credit to the stars," Gabe said. "Columbus ran into America. As long as he was sailing west, he couldn't miss it."

Annie giggled. "I guess you're right. My trip will be the same way. I'll just keep turning right until I get to San Diego. It will be so simple."

He drew her close and kissed the top of her head. "I suppose I can take some solace in that fact. Just as long as you don't steer yourself into a hurricane."

"I promise that if there is a hurricane on the horizon, I'll tie up in port and wait until it passes. Maybe I can call you, and you can come down and wait it out with me."

"That sounds like a good plan." He wasn't going to tell her about the teaching job at the academy or any other options that might pop up. For now, he'd have to find a way to fit into her future rather than fit her into his.

"I CAN'T BELIEVE the weekend is over and you have to go back to North Carolina tomorrow," Annie said.

She and Lisa had taken up residence on the back porch, sprawled out in the heat with tall glasses of lemonade mixed with iced tea. The kids were playing on the lawn in a small paddling pool that Nellie had filled for them, while he and Gabe were down at the boat, trying to rewire the running lights on the mast.

"Couldn't you stay a few more days?"

"I can't," Lisa said.

"But Nellie said you should. He wants you here."

She smiled, then leaned closer. "Promise you won't say a thing? Not even to Gabe?"

"What?" Annie gasped. "You already told us about the baby. So, it's not that. Wait, you're not pregnant with twins, are you?"

"No!" Lisa said, giving her a playful slap. "At least I don't think I am. Oh, God, what if I was? Nellie would flip his lid."

"Then what is it?"

"I have a job interview on Tuesday morning. It's my third interview, and I think there's a good chance I'm going to get it." Lisa laughed and clapped her hands as her excitement bubbled over. "Do you know how long I've waited for this? Now that Nellie has a regular job, we know we'll be staying in the same spot for at least a couple years. After he's done with this project at Pax River, he'll only have to travel a couple times a month."

Annie reached out and gave her friend a hug. "I'm so happy for you. What's the job?"

"It's for a seed company. Vegetables and flowers. I'll be designing their packaging and their displays. Something I can do with a big belly." She reached over the arm of her chair and pulled her tote bag onto her lap. When she found a small notebook, Lisa pushed the bag to her feet and held the book out to her friend.

Annie flipped through it, taking in a mélange of pen and ink drawings, each ablaze with bright color from markers. "Lisa, these are amazing."

"They were just little doodles that I did while I was sitting at the playground, watching the kids. And then, just by luck, I saw the ad online. I showed them my drawings and they loved them. I just have to meet with the president of the company on Tuesday, but they pretty much implied that the job was mine if I wanted it."

"Of course you want it!" Annie cried.

"Of course I do!"

"But why haven't you told Nellie? Do you think he'd disapprove?"

Lisa shook her head. "He's always said it was up to me whether I worked or not. And I know he'll be excited for me. I guess I didn't want to disappoint him, or me, if I didn't get the job. So I decided to wait until it was a sure thing, then we could celebrate."

"I think that's a good idea," Annie said. "Take your time and be sure." She took another sip of her lemonade. "I'm kind of jealous of you. A real job. Maybe you can give me some interview tips."

"Why would you need a job? You have the sailing school. And your trip is coming up. You seem so happy."

Annie nodded. "I am happy. Maybe happier than I've ever been in my life." She paused and grabbed Lisa's hand. "Even happier than I was with Erik."

An uncomfortable silence surrounded them as Annie stared out at the bay. There. She'd said it. The thing that had been nagging at her ever since the weekend began. She'd quietly observed the relationship between Lisa and Nellie, all the while realizing that the trust and intimacy they shared was something she'd never experienced with Erik. She thought she'd loved her husband, but now Annie knew that emotions could run so much deeper between a man and a woman. Gabe was teaching her that.

"I don't know what to say," Lisa murmured.

"You don't have to say anything. Just having you here has made things clearer."

Lisa leaned forward in her chair and grabbed Annie's hand. "You're in love with Gabe, aren't you?"

Annie felt the tears well in her eyes. The response surprised her. She used to cry all the time, but it was always about Erik. "I'm sorry. I don't know why I'm crying."

"Because you're happy?"

Annie laughed through her tears. "Yes. I am happy. And I can't help but feel a little bit guilty about it. Do you think it's too soon?"

"You know how I feel about Gabe," Lisa said. "Of all the men you could have picked, I can't think of a better man to fall in love with."

Annie stood and walked across the porch, then sat down on the rail and observed Lisa's children as they splashed water on each other. A sudden ache twisted at her core, and Annie knew that she wanted children someday, two or three little ones with dark hair and brilliant blue eyes, just like Gabe's.

"When we first started this, it was just supposed to be about a physical relationship," Annie explained in a soft voice. "I was so lonely, and I just wanted someone to touch me, to make me feel alive again. And for a while, that worked. But now, every time I think about my future, I can't help but picture Gabe in it."

"You're in love."

"But I can't fall in love with him. I've already told him that. Lisa, I can't marry another pilot. I can't risk loving a man who might disappear from my life in the blink of an eye. One day Erik was there and the next he wasn't. I never had a chance to tell him that I loved him or to say goodbye. We lost out on so many things."

Lisa got up and joined her at the rail. She smoothed her hand over Annie's back, rubbing gently. "Honey, maybe this is all part of the cosmic plan. Maybe you weren't meant to live your life with Erik. Maybe he was the one who was supposed to lead you to Gabe."

Annie frowned. She'd never considered that possibility. She'd never been very in tune with cosmic matters and only believed in fate or destiny when it came to tragic events. Could Lisa be right?

"I almost asked him to go on my trip with me," Annie said. "But he's signed up for test pilot's school. He starts in February. I'm sure he'd want to stay for that. It's very hard to get a spot."

"You should ask him," Lisa said.

Annie shook her head. "No, I decided I can't. He's already worried about the trip, about me sailing alone. He'd go along just to make sure I was safe, not because he really wanted to go. And I want to do it alone. It's just hard to imagine being away from him for so long."

"You are in love," Lisa said. She got up and slowly

walked back to her chair. "I need to ask you something, and I need you to be completely honest with me."

"What is it?" Annie said, suddenly concerned by the somber expression on her friend's face.

"Do you think Nellie could be cheating on me? I mean, has Gabe ever mentioned anything? Or maybe even Erik?"

"No!" Annie cried.

"Would you tell me if they had?"

"Yes," Annie said. "Yes, I would tell you, if you asked me directly." She paused and observed her friend's expression, an odd feeling coming over her. "This isn't about Nellie, is it?"

"I don't know what you mean," Lisa said. She picked up her glass and drew a deep breath, but Annie could see a slight tremor in her hand. What was she getting at? Did she think that Annie had had an affair with her husband?

"As far as I know, Nellie is not cheating. And he's definitely not cheating with me."

Lisa gasped. "You? You thought I was talking about you?"

"I don't know what you're talking about. This whole conversation is very confusing."

Lisa shook her head. "It's not. Just ask the question. And I'll give *you* an honest answer."

Annie stood, pressing her hand to her chest. Her heart began to race inside her, and she felt a bit lightheaded. Now she understood. This wasn't about Nellie, it was about Gabe. He had been with another woman, and Lisa wanted her to know.

Annie clapped her hands over her ears and shook her head. "No, don't tell me. It doesn't make any difference. We don't have any claims on each other. We're just two consenting adults. Friends with benefits. That's what we are."

Lisa stood and grabbed Annie's wrists, pulling her hands away from her ears. "I'm not talking about Gabe. As far as I know, that man has loved you since the moment he met you. Sure, he's tried to forget you, a few times over the years, with girls who looked strangely like you, I might add. But I can guarantee you that Gabe Pennington is not the kind of guy who cheats."

"Then what—" The question died in Annie's throat. She was talking about Erik. "Oh, I understand."

"If you don't care, I'll forget this ever came up."

"But it's not just you," Annie said. "Nellie knows." A sharp pain pierced her heart. "Does Gabe know?"

"Yeah."

"What does he know?"

"Pretty much everything, I think."

Gabe, the man she'd brought into her bed, the man she'd shared the most incredible intimacies with, had been keeping a secret from her, a secret that made her look like a foolish, naive woman. "I don't want to know," Annie said.

"All right, then," Lisa said. "I'll make sure the boys know. You're right. What difference does it make? Erik is gone. It won't change anything."

"Was it bad? Did everyone know?"

Lisa paused before answering. "He had a reputation. And it was well earned. Even before you guys met. That's why they called him Breaker. For Heartbreaker."

Annie shook her head. "I didn't know that. All that time I was married to him and I didn't know that. I thought it was just one of those radio terms. You know, like, breaker, breaker. Heartbreaker." She brushed an errant tear off her cheek. "How many were there?"

"I don't know. I think there were a lot. It seemed to be a thing with him. He'd go out with the guys and he'd always leave with some woman. There were a few longer affairs. Are you sure you want to hear about this?"

Annie buried her face in her hands. "No. It doesn't make a difference. It's in the past, and I'll just leave it there."

"There is one little thing that's in the present," Lisa said. "Did Erik have a Rolex watch?"

Annie frowned. "Yeah, he did. One day, he was just wearing it. I wondered about it because I knew he'd never spend money on something like that. He told me he won it in a poker game."

"He got it from a woman who stole it from her husband. And now she needs to get it back before her husband finds out it's missing."

Annie jumped up and ran into the house. She stumbled as she rushed up the stairs to her bedroom. The box was on the floor of her closet, filled with the belongings they'd gathered from Erik's locker. Tossing aside the top, she rummaged through the contents until she found the watch. She flipped it over and squinted to read an inscription that didn't make any sense.

Lisa appeared at the door, then crossed the room and sat on the floor next to Annie. She gathered her into an embrace. "It's better that you know," she said softly.

Was it? Annie realized that everything she believed about her marriage had been a lie. And all those years of waiting and worrying while Erik was deployed were for someone she really didn't know.

But there was something worse, something humiliating about the fact that Gabe knew. All along, through all their conversations about Erik and how perfect their marriage had been—he knew. He could have told her, but he'd chosen to let her go on, oblivious to the realities of her world.

"Can we just keep this between the two of us?" Annie asked. "Don't let Nellie know that I know. He'll tell Gabe, and then I'm going to have to discuss it with him."

"I'll just tell Nellie I was snooping around for the watch and found it, and took it without mentioning it to you."

"All right," she said.

Annie drew a ragged breath and leaned back against the wall. All she really wanted to do was crawl into bed, pull the covers over her head and rewind the last nine years of her life. All her memories were suddenly different, colored in a darker hue.

There had been moments when she'd wondered

whether Erik had ever been tempted. They'd even talked about it a few times when she'd felt a distance between them. But he'd always reassured her that their marriage was sound.

She'd trusted a man she'd loved to tell her the truth, and he'd betrayed her. And now Gabe had come into her life and she'd trusted him. Could she afford to make another mistake?

7

"SHE'S A BEAUTY," Nellie said, staring out at the *Honeymoon* as it rocked on anchor. "It's been fun working on her. And fun working with you at the base."

He held out his hand and Gabe grabbed it, giving it a firm shake before pulling his friend into a hug. "Thanks for all your help," Gabe said. "We couldn't have got it done without you."

"How long is the shakedown cruise?"

"I think we'll be out at least three or four days. I've only got a week off. Then I've got that meeting with you and your team out in San Diego. I'll fly out early Friday morning."

"Now that I'm a civilian, I have to fly commercial," Nellie said. "I used to have my own jet to fly."

"If you get in with an airline, you're going to get to fly anywhere in the world. And I'm not doing the flying this time. I'm catching a ride with a Navy transport."

"So, I'll see you then. Have a good time on the

shakedown. And remember to let Annie do all the navigating. Make her prove herself."

"You got it," Gabe said.

"Oh, and one more thing. That little problem we discussed regarding a missing Rolex. It's been solved. Lisa told me that she found it and now has it in her possession. Annie never needs to know."

Gabe breathed a deep sigh of relief. "Thank God," he muttered. "The last thing I wanted to do was tell her the truth about Erik."

"Well, you're in the clear now," Nellie said. "Take care."

Gabe watched as his buddy strode across the lawn to where his car was parked. The school was closed for the week, and tonight was the local Fourth of July celebration. The counselors were sleeping late, and Lisa had left a few hours earlier, the sleeping kids tucked into their seats in the van.

Annie came out onto the porch in time to wish Nellie a good trip back to the base, waving as he drove away. Then she started toward the water's edge, a mug of coffee clutched in her hand. She handed it to Gabe as he pulled her into a quick hug and pressed a kiss to the top of her head.

"Alone at last," he said. He took a sip of his coffee, then turned his gaze to the boat. "I was thinking we might want to install roller furling on the foresail and the mainsail. It will be much easier for you to handle, and you can raise and lower sails from the cockpit. The risk will be less in heavy weather."

Annie shook her head. "Do you know how much a system like that costs?"

"As a matter of fact I do. I ordered one from the outfitter over in Calvert Beach. We can sail over there today and pick it up on our way out."

He thought she'd be pleased, but her expression said otherwise. "No. Absolutely not. I can raise and lower the sails on this boat on my own. And it's just one more thing that could break. What if it goes down? Then I'm stuck trying to disassemble it so I can use the sails the proper way. I don't want it. You can tell them you want your money back."

"All right, all right," Gabe said.

Though they'd both had a good night's sleep, Annie had obviously got up on the wrong side of the bed. He'd never seen her quite so edgy, and he wondered if it had anything to do with the shakedown.

"Everything is going to be fine," he said. "We have most of the electronics installed and—"

"I'm not worried about the boat," she said.

"Then what's the problem? You can talk to me. You can tell me anything."

She gave him a dismissive look, then shook her head. "I need to get some stuff packed. I've made a list of groceries we're going to need. If you want to go into town and get them, that would help. Then I need you to check the charts and make sure they're in the proper order. And you'll need to get ice. I don't want to run down the batteries using the fridge."

"Anything else?" Gabe asked.

"Not that I can think of," Annie replied.

"You're sure? Because, I can think of something you forgot."

"What is that?"

He tossed his coffee mug over his shoulder and reached out to scoop her in his arms. "You forgot to kiss me good morning."

Annie gasped, then wriggled in his arms. "Let me go."

"Not until you kiss me properly," he said. He strode up the steps of the back porch and flung open the screen door, then walked through the kitchen to the table. Spanning her waist with his hands, Gabe set her on the table and parted her legs.

"That's better," he murmured, stepping between them.

She wore a loose cotton dress, and he could tell she wasn't wearing a bra. He smoothed his hands up her thighs, brushing aside the faded fabric, and discovered she'd left her panties behind, as well.

"Oh, dear. Someone forgot their underwear," he teased.

"It was hot this morning."

"Yes, it was. And it's still hot. Some places more than others." He leaned into her, then slipped his hands around her backside and pulled her against him, wrapping her legs around his waist.

Annie leaned back, bracing her arms behind her. "I think you're looking for more than a kiss, sailor."

"Oh, don't call me that," he warned. "I'm a Marine. We don't take kindly to being lumped in with those Navy types."

"But you are going to be a sailor," she said. "You're going to be my first mate. And as first mate, you're going to have to do everything I tell you to."

Gabe chuckled and gave her a brisk salute. "What's your first order, Captain?"

"Go lock the door," she said. "And make it quick."

When he returned to the table, she was watching him with a wicked smile curling her lips. Her pale hair was tousled, as if she'd combed it with her fingers. "I see your mood has improved," he murmured.

Annie reached for the button at the waist of his cargo shorts. "Where did you sleep last night?" she asked.

"In the hammock on the porch. We worked on programming the navigation system until after midnight. By that time, you were asleep on the sofa. I didn't want to wake you."

She flipped open the button, then slowly drew the zipper down. He held his breath as she reached inside his shorts and pulled out his cock, already hot and swollen. "What are you going to do with that?" he murmured, his gaze fixed on the way her fingers wrapped around him and gently stroked.

With her free hand, she dragged her skirt up along her thigh, exposing herself. "I think we better put it away."

Gabe chuckled softly, grabbing hold of her legs and pulling her close. He didn't bother with foreplay. There would be plenty of time for that later. Right now, he wanted to feel the warmth of her body surround him, a sensation that he'd found tantalizingly addictive as of late. That moment, when they became one, and then the moments that followed as he lost himself inside her, inch by inch.

He began to move, very slowly at first, plunging deep and then withdrawing until they barely touched. His hands smoothed along the length of her bare legs, her skin silken and warm.

Gabe grabbed her foot and pressed his lips to the arch below her ankle. The shift in her position created an interesting friction, and he slowly brought her leg up to rest on his shoulder.

A moan slipped from her lips and Gabe smiled, his own pleasure increasing with hers. There might come a time when this would be nothing but a fantasy, a hazy memory of a stolen summer. He wanted to remember every sensation, every image of her beautiful face and lovely body as he brought her closer to the edge.

He reached out and pulled the front of her dress down, exposing a perfect breast. Cupping the warm flesh with his hand, he ran his thumb over her nipple, drawing it to a peak before he moved on.

He'd explored every inch of her body, from her nape to the arch of her foot. He knew every mole and freckle and could recall them at will. But it was the woman inside who would always fascinate him. He'd never fully know her, or understand her, but that was part of the mystery that kept him coming back.

She arched against the table, her hand clutching his forearm. Gabe reached between them and touched her, knowing the exact spot that brought her the most pleasure. He saw the change in her expression almost immediately, a smile playing at her lips as she murmured his name.

He made it last as long as he could. There were times when he couldn't hold back, when the first contact brought him right to the edge. And there were other times when he could bring her to multiple orgasms before he succumbed himself. This time he'd been on edge from the start.

When she finally tensed beneath his touch, Gabe knew that it was nearly over. And then, a few seconds later, he felt the waves of spasms course through her body. Annie cried out as he increased his pace.

And then Gabe was there, erupting inside her, each sensation timed with a thrust until there was nothing left for him to do but collapse on top of her, breathless and satisfied.

How many more times would they enjoy these pleasures? They had six weeks by the calendar. Would it be enough?

Living without her was something he'd learn to accept, but there was no way he could stop loving her. From that very first kiss, he'd known that there was no other woman for him. Hell, that feeling went back to the first time he set eyes on her. He'd been carrying a torch for almost a third of his life.

Now he finally had a chance to build a life with this woman, to show her what their life together could be. It didn't matter that she'd be gone for months, or maybe even a year. He was used to waiting. But as certain as he was about his feelings, Gabe had no idea how she felt about him.

"I sure like this more than swabbing the decks, Captain Annie."

"Arrrgghh," she said.

It was enough to set him off. He began to laugh and he couldn't stop. Bracing his hands on either side of her body, he pushed up. Her eyes were closed, but she was still smiling. "Is there anything else I can do for you?"

"Take me back to bed," she said.

"We need to get ready to leave," he said.

"That can wait. I just need a few more hours of sleep. Then, I promise, we'll go."

"You can rest," he said. "I'll get things set up for us."

"Are you disobeying your captain, swabbie?"

"You sound just like a pirate," he said, laughing at the silly accent she'd adopted.

"Take me to bed or I'll make you walk the plank," she shouted. "Where's my parrot? I'm supposed to have a parrot."

Gabe picked her up, wrapping her legs around his waist and carrying her through the kitchen. He struggled with the stairs, and by the time they reached her bed, he fell into the tangle of pillows and blankets.

Her edgy mood had dissolved, replaced by the sweet and funny Annie he'd come to know so well. She snuggled up beside him, his chin resting on her shoulder, his leg thrown across her thighs. "I'm not sure I'm the right boy for this job."

"Oh, don't worry," Annie said, her voice soft. "You're perfect."

ANNIE SLOWLY OPENED her eyes and squinted at the clock on the bedside table. At first, she thought it read 8:00 a.m. She'd been sleeping for less than an hour. She groaned softly, then rolled over, pulling the pillow over her face.

Gabe must have waited until she fell asleep before he made his escape and went back to work. She reached out and felt his side of the bed. It was cold and empty. She looked at the clock again, then sat up and rubbed her eyes. It wasn't 8:00 a.m., it was 3:00 p.m.

She threw the sheet off her body. She was still in the dress she'd put on that morning, the skirt twisted around her waist and the buttons down the front undone. Annie raked her hands through her tangled hair, then buttoned her dress as she raced downstairs.

"Gabe?" she called, her voice echoing through the house.

The screen door slammed behind her, and she squinted against the afternoon sun. She caught sight of him down along the water and hurried to the spot, her feet bare in the cool grass. "Gabe!"

He turned away from the dinghy and waved as she approached. "Hey. You're up!"

"Why did you let me sleep? It's past three. We should have left hours ago."

"You were obviously tired. I thought it would be best for you to get some sleep while I got us ready to go." He braced his hands on his hips. "And you're angry again."

"Again?"

"You were mad at me this morning for something.

Never did figure that out. And now you're pissed again."

"I don't like it when you make decisions for me. I wanted to help get things ready. It's my boat. My trip. And my responsibility."

"I was doing you a favor."

"No, you weren't. You were taking care of me, just like you've been doing ever since you started coming out here. You bought all this stuff for the boat, stuff I didn't need. And you're buying groceries and bringing dinner home. And mowing the lawn and fixing my car."

He cursed, then shook his head. "And what the hell is wrong with that? I thought you'd appreciate the help."

He'd never once raised his voice to her, but this time, she'd pushed him too far. Annie knew she was being ungrateful. But she couldn't let him continue to dominate her life like this. He was making all the decisions and cloaking them behind the guise of just helping her out.

She wasn't even going to bring up the issue of Erik's infidelities. He'd let her go on and on about what a wonderful husband he'd been, how hard it was for her to move on and begin a new life. And all the while he knew that Erik had been making a fool of her.

Even now, nearly two years later, she still felt humiliated. "This is my trip," she said. "I planned it. I've been thinking about it for a long time. I want to set the boat up my way. I want to stow the provisions and get the sails ready. I want to take care of all the details."

"You're right," he said. "I overstepped. I'll leave you to take care of this." He turned and dragged the dinghy to the edge of the water, then stepped in.

"Where are you going?"

"I'm going to unload everything I loaded earlier. So you can do it your way. It's going to take me a while, but the way I figure, you should be able to shove off sometime after midnight. I'll set my alarm, and I'll come down and wave goodbye."

"What? You're not coming with anymore?"

He shook his head. "Naw, I can't. I'd just have to sit around and try not to help you out. It wouldn't be much fun now, would it?"

"Fine!" Annie shouted. "I'd rather do it myself anyway." She watched him as he crawled out of the dinghy.

"On second thought, you can unload all the stuff I loaded. I'm going to take the rest of the after-noon off." He strode back to the house. But when he stopped halfway, Annie held her breath.

He started back toward her and stopped twice before crossing the distance. "You know, all I've ever wanted to do was love you. Even when you were in love with my best friend, you were the only woman I thought about. And I knew, if I just had a chance, I could make this work. But I have to say…" He shook his head, as if he couldn't go on. "I have to say that I was wrong. I can't make you love me. No matter how hard I try to show you that I care, you just can't see it. Yes, you had a perfect marriage, and those don't come along every day. And you don't want to fall in love with someone in the military. I can understand that, too. But you're never going to find anyone else who loves you the way I do. And that's a fact."

"Are you finished?" she asked.

"No, I'm not. There's something else." He walked over to the pile of supplies that sat next to the dinghy. He rummaged through a canvas bag until he came up with a small gift, wrapped in shiny paper and festooned with a bow.

"This is for you," he said. "It's a present. People who like each other give each other presents. Not all presents are sexual by the way."

"Very funny," she said, turning the package over in her hands.

"Open it," he said.

She fumbled with the ribbon, letting it drop to the grass, then tore the paper away from a beautiful leather journal. He'd had her name embossed on the front, with the name of her boat just below that. Tucked inside the front was a package of her favorite pens.

Annie looked up at him, and he gave her a rueful smile. "I thought that you could write about your adventure, and then I could read about it when you got home." He shoved his hand in his pocket and pulled out a wrinkled envelope. "And there's this. It's probably going to make you really angry, but I'll give it to you anyway. If you don't want to do it, you can just throw it out."

Annie stared down at the envelope. The logo of a popular sailing magazine was printed on the outside. She withdrew a letter and scanned the contents.

We would be delighted to discuss a freelance assignment with Ms. Jennings to appear regularly in our Wanderings section of the magazine. Please have her contact us at her earliest convenience.

She glanced up at Gabe. "You did this?"

"They're going to pay you," he said, pointing to the last paragraph. "Ten cents a word. It's not a lot, but it will help pay for the trip."

Annie felt tears push at the corners of her eyes. Why was it so hard for her to accept his help? Was it because she'd have to accept his love at the same time? She'd already decided that she was falling in love with him, so why wasn't he allowed to reciprocate?

Annie had tried to work it out in her head, but she couldn't seem to find an explanation. They slept next to each other every night, they made love until the early-morning hours. She'd never been closer to a man. But to allow him to love her would…would—What would it do?

Annie brushed a tear from her cheek. "Thank you," she said. "I…I'm sorry about what I—"

He reached out and pressed his finger to her lips. "Don't worry. I understand."

Annie shook her head. How could he understand when she didn't? "Do you?"

"Not really. I'm not sure I'll ever understand you completely. But maybe that's the fascination. There'll always be something new to learn." Gabe took a step back. "I have to get back to the base. Good luck with the shakedown cruise."

"What? You're just going to walk away?" Annie bit back a sob, refusing to let her tears take hold.

Gabe turned to face her and held his arms up in mock surrender. "Yeah, I am. You don't need me, Annie. I don't need you. We're just wasting time here."

Annie watched him go, defiantly holding her tears back. It was no use. It was bound to end sooner or later. Friends with benefits only worked if both parties remained friends, and Gabe had never been satisfied with being just her friend.

She turned and looked at the provisions scattered around the dinghy. There was nothing there that she really needed. She could find food along the way. Drawing a deep breath, she walked to the water's edge and waded in. With strong strokes, she swam to the *Honeymoon*. Crawling up the swim ladder on the stern, she looked back at the house.

He was gone. She'd driven him away. And now she was alone again. Annie smoothed the water out of her hair, then began to prepare to set sail. The steps were second nature to her—anchor line, foresail up, adjust the rudder, winch the lines.

She worked efficiently, falling into a rhythm that

soothed her nerves. Within minutes, the boat was skimming over the surface of the water, headed out into the bay, the wind at her back. With a litany of tasks ahead of her, she could clear her mind.

Annie didn't have to think about Gabe and the argument they'd just had. She didn't have to wonder how he felt about her or whether what she felt for him was really love. She could just turn her face into the sun and let the breeze blow through her hair.

There were all sorts of possibilities just waiting over the horizon. Gabe had helped her feel alive again, and she was grateful for that. But from now on, Annie was going to steer her own course.

"I THINK IF you switch the control to this panel, it makes more sense. It's more intuitive to the pilot, and it follows the same pattern as the other systems in the cockpit. Little things like that save reaction time in a combat situation."

Jim Bowlin, the lead engineer on the project, nodded. "All right, Captain. I'll write up the change and send it in."

"Great." Gabe glanced at his watch. It was three thirty on a Friday afternoon. On any normal week, he'd be planning to sneak out early and head up the western shore to Annie's place. But since last weekend, they hadn't spoken.

She'd taken off on the boat, leaving behind half of the provisions that they'd bought. Gabe had waited around until the next morning, hoping that she'd just taken the boat down the coast and dropped anchor a few miles away. He'd called one of the counselors every day in the late afternoon, but she hadn't returned.

"You have plans for the weekend?"

Gabe looked up at Bowlin, who was going through a sheaf of papers on a clipboard. "No. Nothing important."

This was what it would be like when Annie was on her trip. Day after day of wondering where she was and what she was doing. She was still in American waters, so at least he knew she was relatively safe. But he'd checked the weather last night and there were some heavy storms due to move through Chesapeake Bay and the counties surrounding it.

"Captain Pennington?" A young woman dressed in a naval uniform strode through the hangar. Her nameplate designated her as Ensign Sheffer. "Are you Captain Pennington?"

"I am," Gabe said.

She handed him a box. "This was delivered to you an hour ago."

Gabe opened the box and pulled aside tissue paper, then withdrew a stuffed parrot. He glanced up to find Bowlin and Sheffer watching him, bemused expressions on their faces. "It's a stuffed parrot," Gabe said. "It's an inside joke. At least I think it is."

Gabe searched the box for a note and found it beneath the tissue paper, along with a black eye patch. He withdrew the note. "Slip 64, Back Creek Marina in Johnstown. Dinner at 6. Wear the eye patch."

He chuckled softly and held up the eye patch. "I guess I do have dinner plans after all," he said.

Gabe spent the next half hour finishing up paperwork, then headed to the barracks to take a quick shower and change out of his uniform into civvies. He left the base and stopped to get a bottle of wine in Johnstown before making his way to the marina.

It was only 5:00 p.m., an hour before the time he was supposed to arrive, but Gabe didn't care. He'd been away from Annie for five days, and he wasn't sure when she'd be leaving. He was going to take all the time he could get.

As he slowly made his way through the marina, his eyes scanned the boats, looking for the *Honeymoon*. He found her mast, and the distinctive flag of the sailing school fluttering in the wind.

She was exactly where she said she'd be, and as he approached, he slowed his step to watch her. Annie, dressed in shorts and a bikini top, was scrubbing the deck with a long-handled brush and a hose. In just a week, her pale hair had lightened a few shades, and her skin had tanned more deeply.

In just a week, she looked so different. Would she feel different in his arms? She'd had five days to think about everything that had happened between them. Had anything changed? Gabe was almost afraid to approach. He'd been the one to drive her away, and he'd had to suffer the consequences.

"Ahoy!" he shouted.

Annie straightened, her eyes hidden behind her sunglasses. He couldn't read her expression. Was she smiling? She waved at him, then dropped the brush and jumped off the deck onto the pier.

They met where the main pier intersected with the finger pier. He stood on the step above her, the parrot dangling from his hand. Gabe held it up. "Is this your bird?"

She nodded. "He's been keeping me company."

Annie grabbed the parrot and pulled a small ring near his neck. "Awk, walk the plank, matey," the bird said.

"He's not quite the conversationalist that you are, but he doesn't boss me around."

"Yeah, well, I'm not going to apologize for caring about you. Besides, I can do a lot of things that parrot can't do, if you know what I mean."

"You underestimate the parrot," she said with a smile.

"I can unstuff that bird in a matter of seconds," Gabe warned. He bent down and cupped her cheek in his hand, then brushed a quick kiss across her lips. She didn't draw away or look as if the kiss was unwanted, and Gabe took some solace in that fact. "I didn't expect to see you this soon."

"I had a lot of time to think and I just didn't like leaving that way. We've shared a lot this summer and you deserved a much nicer farewell. So, here I am, parrot in hand, hoping you'll accept my apology. It would be bad karma to start a voyage with such negative feelings, don't you think?"

"I do. And I accept your apology." He bent close and kissed her again, a sweet, simple kiss that telegraphed nothing of his need for her. "How's it been going? Is everything working?"

Annie nodded. "I had some trouble with the autopilot, but I think I got it fixed. And I'm reconsidering the roller furling. It would be good for heavy weather."

"I think that would be a good idea," Gabe said.

He wanted to pull her into his arms and kiss her until they were both aching for more. But there seemed to be an invisible wall between them now, holding them at a polite distance.

"Is that a bottle of wine in that bag?" Annie asked.

"It is. What do you say we open it and have a glass."

"Come on," she said, turning to head to the boat. "I don't have any wineglasses, but I do have some nice plastic cups."

He sat in the cockpit while Annie went below to grab a corkscrew and the cups. She returned with a plate of cheese and crackers, setting it down on the bench between them. Gabe opened the wine and poured them both a cup.

"To fair winds and calm seas," he said, touching his cup to hers.

"Actually, I've been hoping for some rough weather," Annie said. "You really can't test the boat unless you get it out in high winds and rough water."

He wasn't about to tell her that a storm would roll in later that evening. If she wanted to know that, then she could damn well check the weather service on her own.

"I thought you were going to head into port if there was rough weather," Gabe said.

"Yeah, but that's not for some squall or thunderstorm," she said. "I was talking about a hurricane. I can handle a storm that lasts an hour or two."

"As much as I want to believe in your sailing abilities, I think you need to remember that you'll be alone. It's a lot harder."

"I know. But I've sailed in bad weather before. I know what I'm doing."

He held his tongue. It didn't matter what he thought. She was determined to do what she wanted to do. From now on, it was apparent that he'd be along for the ride. She was the one in the driver's seat.

Still, he had a few aces up his sleeve, and Gabe decided to use a few of them now, hoping to see if his potential plans might have an effect on her. "I know Nellie told you that I've been accepted into test pilot's school."

She nodded. "He did. And that's wonderful. That should help if you want to be an astronaut," Annie said.

"Or a teacher," he said.

"A teacher?"

"I've also been approached to teach at the naval academy. I'd have to go back to school and get a doctorate. But I've already applied to a few universities and I've sent them my master's thesis."

"So, what are you going to do?" Annie asked.

"I don't know. I guess I'm going to have to decide whether I want to give up flying or not. As a test pilot,

I'll keep flying, but it won't be in combat situations. I guess both of us have a lot of decisions to make."

"I did make one decision while I was sailing around on the Chesapeake," Annie said.

He wasn't sure he wanted to hear what she had to say. In truth, he knew from the way she was behaving that it wasn't anything good. With the exception of the brief kiss they'd shared, she hadn't touched him since he'd stepped on the boat. A week ago, they couldn't keep their hands off each other.

Gabe took a long gulp of his wine and pasted a smile on his face. "And what did you decide?"

"I think that maybe it was a mistake for me to ask you to do the whole friends with benefits thing."

"Why is that?" Gabe asked.

"Because we've never really had a chance to be friends," she said. "We didn't have a chance to get to know each other before we became intimate. And I think that some of the problems we're having now are because of that. Maybe if we'd been friends first, we wouldn't have decided to become lovers."

"What are you saying?"

"I'm saying that maybe we should begin again—as friends."

"Well, that might work for you," Gabe said, an edge of anger in his voice. "But it won't for me. I can't just throw my feelings into reverse because you want something different."

"Please, don't be mad. I know—"

"You don't know," he said. "And that's because I

never had the courage to tell you. I love you, Annie. It's as simple as that. I love you."

She drew her feet up and wrapped her arms around her legs, resting her chin on her knees. "How can I believe that? How can I ever trust those words again?"

"You can trust them because they're coming from me."

"Can I?" she asked.

"Why not? What have I ever done to make you doubt my feelings?"

"I know that Erik cheated on me. I know that you knew, along with a few hundred other friends and associates. I know about the major's wife and the Rolex."

Gabe drew in a deep breath. He hadn't expected this. He wasn't prepared to explain himself on that particular subject. "How did you find out?"

"Lisa told me. The question is, why didn't you tell me? If you loved me, like you say you do, then how could you keep a secret like that?"

"Are you kidding? It was a lose-lose situation. I didn't want to hurt you. I know how much you loved and trusted him, and I didn't want to destroy your memory of him. I didn't want you to hate me. I can list another twenty reasons if you'd like. What difference does it make now? It's in the past."

"It doesn't feel like it's in the past," Annie said, her voice soft. "It hurts right now."

Gabe reached out and took her hand in his, drawing her fingers to his lips. "What do you want me to do?" he murmured.

"I want us to forget the whole friends with benefits deal and be just friends. No benefits."

Though it was exactly what he expected, her request felt like a punch to the gut. After all they'd shared, she was willing to just toss it aside as if it didn't mean anything. As if he didn't mean anything.

Maybe this wasn't what he wanted, Gabe mused. But it was what he deserved. This was punishment for breaking the bro code. He'd pursued the wife of his best friend. And though Erik was gone, and had given Gabe permission to watch over Annie, it still wasn't right. It had felt like a betrayal from the start. Gabe had just refused to recognize it.

"I think you're right," he finally said. "This was doomed to fail from the start."

"I…I wouldn't say that," Annie countered.

Gabe set his cup on the bench and got to his feet. "I'm glad we had this chance to talk," he said. "I know this will be better for you. And better for me."

"Gabe, don't go. Let's have dinner. We can talk," Annie said.

"There's nothing to talk about. I understand how you feel, Annie. And you're aware of how I feel. You need to find your own way before you can commit to any kind of relationship. And I have a lot of choices to make, too. I think I'm going to need more than a nice dinner and some friendly conversation to get adjusted to this new dynamic."

He jumped up onto the dock, then turned to take one last look at her. No matter what women came into his life in the future, she would remain the most beautiful woman he'd ever known. "I can't just stop loving you, Annie. The truth is, I don't want to. I need you in my life. I want the whole thing, the happily-ever-after, and I'm not willing to settle for less. You may think that's selfish, and maybe it is. But I knew I'd probably only have one chance to convince you that we'd be good together. And somehow, I managed to blow it. I can live with that because at least I gave it my best."

Satisfied that he'd said everything that needed saying, Gabe turned and strode down the dock. She called his name twice, but she didn't come after him. When he got to his car, he sat behind the wheel for a full minute before he could start the engine.

It was better this way, he said to himself. She was never going to love him, no matter what he did. Any chance they might have at a future was impossible. The sooner he moved on, the better.

8

ANNIE SAT ON the porch swing and stared down at a blank sheet of paper, all she'd had to show after an hour of trying to write her first contribution to the Wanderings column for *Topsail* magazine. They'd wanted an article for the September issue, and since she'd start her trip in September, they wanted her to talk about herself, her reasons for taking the cruise and the setup of the *Honeymoon*.

She'd arrived home a week ago, just hours before the next class of student sailors had begun to arrive for the third session. The counselors had kept the camp in shape while she was gone, completing a long list of tasks she'd left them along with enjoying seven days of freedom.

Annie stared out at the water, at her boat bobbing at anchor, then glanced down at the pad of paper. She'd been trying to start her article for the last hour but couldn't seem to come up with a suitable first line.

Her mind was such a tangle of emotions, she couldn't sort it all out, at least not enough to make sense of it.

In another month, she'd be gone, sailing away from the comfort of a soft bed and running water. The first leg of the trip was simple. A thousand miles in the protection of the Intercoastal Waterway. But Annie was starting to reconsider that part of the plan. If she sailed on open ocean, still keeping close to the shore, she could make better time. And if the hurricane season stirred up some storms, she could duck into a nearby harbor and wait out the weather.

She'd dreamed about this trip for many years, but before Erik's death, she'd always pictured the two of them together, working the sails, strolling through quaint villages, making love on the deck at night under a starry sky.

Those images barely surfaced in her mind anymore. In truth, she found herself thinking of what it might be like to have Gabe along on the trip. Not that she was afraid of the task she faced, but he always was such good company. When she felt down, he always had a way to brighten her mood. She felt like a better version of herself when they were together. At least she had until their last encounter.

Why did it have to end that way? Why couldn't she have just allowed him the pleasure of loving her for as long as he wanted? What harm could there be in his feelings? And why did she feel the need to reject him so completely? So many questions. And not a single sensible answer to any of them.

It had been almost two weeks since she'd said

goodbye to Gabe, and in that time, there had been no word, no call. Nothing to give her a clue as to how he was doing. Maybe that was for the best. If he was miserable, she'd probably be racked with guilt for her part in it. And if he was blissfully happy with a new woman in his life, she'd be left to question whether she'd made the biggest mistake in her own life.

Annie reached out and picked up her journal, the one Gabe had given her as a gift. She smoothed her fingertips over the gold-embossed cover and smiled. If it weren't for Gabe, she wouldn't have the writing job with *Topsail*, or sponsors willing to provide her with sails and foul-weather gear and an emergency radio beacon.

He'd worked on the boat as if it were his own, and she'd never really thanked him properly. In truth, he'd done so much for her in such a short time that she felt positively ungrateful and selfish for not finding a way to express her gratitude.

Annie reached for her cell phone and brought up Gabe's number. But she couldn't bring herself to push the button to dial it. What would she say to him? They'd shared so much in such a short time, and now they were back to being strangers.

A car horn broke the sleepy silence of the afternoon, and Annie's heart leaped when she realized that all the counselors were still in camp. She got up from the swing and wandered to the far end of the porch, peering around the edge of the house to find a familiar van approaching.

Annie ran to the steps, then circled the house, end-ing up at the driveway just as Lisa pulled the van to a stop. She pulled open the driver's door and dragged her friend out, drawing her into a fierce hug.

"What are you doing here?" Annie cried. "Why didn't you call?"

"I knew you'd be here as long as the sailing school was in session," Lisa said. "And I wanted to surprise you."

"I needed a nice surprise," Annie said, pulling her into another hug.

"I figured you might. Nellie said that you and Gabe have stopped seeing each other."

"I told him I just wanted to be friends, and I guess he didn't want that, because he just stopped any kind of contact. He hasn't called or written. I don't know where he is or what he's doing." Annie shook her head. "I don't want to talk about him. Let's talk about you. Why are you here?"

"Nellie had to come up to Pax River to finish up the project he was working on with Gabe. Then he and I are going to have a nice little weekend in DC, away from our three lovely children and our adorable dog. It's our last chance before I start to blow up like a balloon."

"Come," Annie said. "Sit down on the porch and I'll get us some drinks. What would you like? Iced tea? Or I have some raspberry lemonade."

"Iced tea is good for me," Lisa said. "Though I'd truly crave a glass of wine."

Annie giggled. "All right. Iced tea for both of us." She hurried into the kitchen and poured two glasses of tea from the huge pitcher she kept in the fridge. She added sugar and a few slices of lemon, then returned to the porch. Lisa was stretched out in one of the old wicker rockers. Annie handed her a glass, then sat down beside her.

"You look so beautiful. It's true what they say, about pregnant women having a glow about them."

"Oh, please. That glow is sweat and it comes from six hours in a van with no air-conditioning." Lisa took a sip of her tea. "Do you want to tell me how you managed to screw things up with Gabe Pennington? Or would you prefer to talk about my swollen ankles?"

"Why do you think it was me?"

"Because that man would do anything for you, and I mean anything. There's no way he would have messed it up. It must have been you."

"I just wasn't ready," Annie said. "It all happened so fast, and it felt as if he was trying to pull me away from all of these plans that I'd made." She paused. "I got married so young, and after Erik died, I had no idea who I was. I was finally starting to figure it out, and then I found out that my marriage was a complete lie. I didn't want to start living my life for another man, just to have it happen all over again."

"Guys like Gabe don't come along very often," Lisa said. "He's crazy about you. He'll treat you like a princess. I know it sounds silly, but that kind of love is something you can build a life around."

"What if I don't feel the same way?" Annie asked.

Lisa groaned. "Don't be silly. I know you love him. I can see it in the way your face lights up when you talk about him. And how you say his name. Annie Foster Jennings, do not mess this up!"

"I'm not sure I want to get married again."

"What about children?"

"You weren't married when you had your kids. And you raised them as a single mother for most of their lives. It can be done."

"Why would you want to do it when you can have a guy like Gabe to—"

"A guy like Gabe, a guy like Gabe. What if he turns out to be a guy like Erik? A guy who cheats and then turns around and tells me how much he loves me."

"Gabe wouldn't do that. He's waited too long to risk losing you."

Annie held out her hand to stop Lisa. "Can we talk about something else? Thinking about him just makes me more confused."

"All right. But I do plan to return to the subject before I leave."

"Oh, goody," Annie said, taking a long drink of her tea.

Lisa's cell phone rang, and she pulled it out of her purse. "Oh, a text from my hubby. He misses me already. Isn't that—" The smile slowly faded.

"What is it?"

"Nellie says that Gabe's been in an accident. They've taken him to the hospital on the base. He says we should come right away."

For a moment, Annie couldn't speak. Her throat had

gone dry and her mind was frozen. "Was it a crash?" Annie finally asked, tears welling up in her eyes.

Lisa shook her head. "He doesn't say. He says 'surgery within the hour.'"

"Let me just let the counselors know where I'm going and I'll—"

"I'll let them know," Lisa said. "You go change and throw some things in a bag. You might want to stay overnight. I'll see if I can get more information out of Nellie."

Annie hurried back into the house, still clutching her iced tea. She tossed the glass into the sink and it shattered. When she reached her bedroom, her pulse was pounding so hard she could barely think.

Her mind wound back to the day she'd found out about Erik. They'd sent someone from the base. The officer had stood on her front porch and explained what had happened, how Erik had died in service to his country. "Gabe's not dead," Annie murmured to herself. "He can't die."

She threw some clothes into a bag and rushed back downstairs. Two of the counselors stood in the kitchen with Lisa, and Annie paused. "Take the kids for pizza tonight like we planned," she said. "Sarah will be in to cook the meals tomorrow, so you should be set. Call me on my cell if you need me. And please don't let anyone get hurt or drown. Promise me?"

The two counselors nodded. "Will you let us know how he is?"

"I will," Lisa said. She grabbed Annie's bag. "I'll

wait for you in the van. And I'll call Nellie to see if I can get more information from him."

"I'll be right out," Annie said. She gave the counselors a few more instructions, then hurried outside to join Lisa.

When she got in the van, Annie looked to her friend for more news, but Lisa shook her head. "He's not answering. But that doesn't mean anything. He might have had to turn his phone off because he was in the hospital."

"Right. That's probably it." As they sped out to the highway, Annie tried to keep her thoughts positive. An accident. He could have sprained his ankle or bumped his head. But then, that wouldn't require surgery, would it?

"This doesn't mean that I love him," Annie said, her gaze fixed on the road ahead. "He's a good friend and I'm concerned about his well-being, that's all."

"I know that's what you're telling yourself," Lisa said. "But I think you're full of doo-doo."

"Doo-doo?" Annie giggled. "Really? I'm full of doo-doo?"

"We try not to swear in our household. And now that Nellie is home nearly full-time, it's getting a lot harder. I just think you should stop being a poop-head and admit that you've been wrong about Gabe. Admit that you're in love with him."

Annie wrapped her arms around herself, a shiver coursing through her body. She felt as if she couldn't catch her breath, and she'd grown light-headed. "I'm feeling a little dizzy."

"Put your head between your knees," Lisa said. "And take long, deep breathes."

Annie did as she was told, bumping her head on the glove compartment as she went down. "Ouch," she cried, rubbing her head. She stared at her toes, painted a pretty shade of pink, as she moderated her breathing. Within a few minutes, the panic had subsided, but the feeling of dread was still there.

"How long will it take to get there?" Annie asked.

"It took me fifty minutes to drive the distance this morning. If I drive a little faster, I suppose forty or forty-five minutes."

"How long have we been gone?" Annie asked.

"About five minutes. Just sit back and relax."

Relax, Annie thought to herself. It was an impossible task when all she could think about was Gabe Pennington, lying in a hospital bed, close to death, his own feelings still bottled up inside him.

Annie said a silent prayer and then made a deal with God. If He spared Gabe, then she would forget her plans to sail to San Diego and allow herself to fall in love.

GABE OPENED HIS eyes to a hazy world of beeping machines and harsh white lights. He reached up to rub his forehead but found his right wrist enclosed in a splint. He wiggled his fingers, but there was no pain.

When he pulled up his left arm, he found tubes taped to the skin on the back of his hand. Pushing up on his elbows, he examined the rest of his body.

"Shit," he muttered when his saw his right leg enclosed in a plaster cast.

"Gabe?"

The sound of Annie's voice cleared the cobwebs from his head, and he turned to find her sitting in a chair on the other side of the bed. She stood and crossed the room to stand beside the bed.

"You gave me quite a scare," Annie said.

"What are you doing here?"

"Nellie called. He said you'd had an accident and you needed surgery."

"What happened?" he asked.

"You were on a ladder doing something to the helicopter and you lost your balance," Annie explained.

He watched as her eyes filled with tears. "Hey, why are you crying? It's not your fault I'm a klutz. It could happen to anyone. And it's not the first broken limb I've had. I broke my arm once after a hard landing and my ankle when my chopper ran headfirst into an embankment." He glanced down at his leg. "It looks like the doctors fixed me up pretty well."

Annie smiled, brushing away the tears. "You do sound like you're feeling all right."

"Massive amounts of painkiller, I think," Gabe said. "I'm pretty sure that's what this little button is for." He held it out to her. "Should we give it a try?"

A nurse strode into the room, holding an electronic notepad in her hand. "Captain Pennington, good to see that you're awake. How are you feeling?"

"Good. What time is it?"

"It's half past eight," the nurse said.

Gabe frowned. "Morning or night?"

"Night," she said. "The painkillers have kept you sleeping for most of the afternoon, and now that the anesthesia has worn off, it's time for you to get up and get moving."

"My leg is broken."

"In two places. They had to put in a couple plates and some screws to stabilize the bone. But you should heal quickly. The physical therapist will be here in a few minutes to give you some crutches, and then we'll get you moving."

"Is everything else all right?" Annie asked.

"Is this your wife?" the nurse asked.

"Yes," he said, and the same time Annie said, "No."

"Which is it?"

"She's my girlfriend," Gabe said.

Annie gave him an odd look, and Gabe shrugged. "And you can tell her whatever information you tell me. How long am I going to need this cast?"

"The doctor will give you that information," she said. "He'll be in tomorrow morning. And he'll be able to tell you when you might be going home, as well."

"If you had to guess, when might that be?" Gabe asked.

"If you're getting along on crutches, it could be as early as tomorrow. I guess I don't need to ask if you have someone who can take care of you."

"No," Annie said. "You don't need to ask."

After the nurse left the room, Gabe patted the edge

of the bed, and Annie sat down next to him. "You're not going to have to take care of me. I'll figure out a way to get by."

"No, I want to. I owe it to you. You've done so much for me this summer and I—"

"It's not a debt that has to be paid," Gabe said. "That's not why I did those things. Besides, you have plans at the end of the month."

"I don't have to leave right away," she said. "It would probably be better if I waited anyway."

Gabe shook his head. "No. I plan to stand on the shore and wave goodbye as you sail out into the Chesapeake. After all the work we put in on the boat, I'm counting on it."

She nodded and forced a smile. "All right. If that's what you want."

He saw the relief on her face, and Gabe knew that the lie had worked. His feelings about the trip hadn't changed, but his feeling for Annie had.

In the time they'd spent apart, he'd realized that loving a woman as bright and capable and determined as Annie would come with some challenges. She was also fiercely independent. And if he truly loved her, then he'd have to let her exercise that independence whenever she wanted to.

It was one of those qualities that he loved in her. There were far too many to list, but with time and distance, he was beginning to understand what made her so attractive.

"I could go get you something to eat," Annie said.

"They'll probably bring me dinner at some point," he said. "Unless I slept through it."

"Knock, knock."

They both looked to the door to see Nellie and Lisa at the door. They both carried bags from a local restaurant, and Nellie set them on a nearby tray table and began to unpack the contents.

"We figured you'd be hungry, so we picked up some sandwiches and a few other goodies."

"Weren't you two supposed to be on your way to DC for the weekend?"

"We can't leave you stranded here," Lisa said.

Gabe chuckled. "I'm not alone. Annie is here."

"I'll be fine," Annie said. "You guys need to go."

Lisa looked at her husband and shrugged. "I suppose if we left now, we'd still be able to get our room."

Nellie nodded, then grabbed her hand. But Lisa stopped him as he pulled her to the door. She reached in her pocket and tossed Annie her keys. "We'll pick it up on Sunday evening," she said.

Annie tucked the keys in the pocket of her jacket. "Thanks," she said.

"Take good care of him," Nellie said.

A few moments later, the room was silent. Gabe wasn't sure what to do. He wanted to reach out and pull Annie into his arms, to kiss her like he'd kissed her in the past. But he was no longer certain she'd respond.

There seemed to be a wall standing between them, thicker and stronger than anything that had come between them in the past. He sensed that it wouldn't come down with kisses or sweet promises or even just the simple truth.

"I never got to say goodbye to him," Annie murmured, staring out the window at the setting sun.

"Nellie? I'm sure he doesn't mind."

"No, Erik. One minute, he was part of my life, and the next minute, he was gone. I thought I would have felt it or sensed it somehow. But I didn't."

"It doesn't always happen that way," Gabe said.

"We fought the last morning we were together," Annie said. "It was a real barn burner. And after he left, I was so angry that I decided I'd give him an ultimatum. He either left active duty after his tour was up or I'd divorce him. Did he ever say anything to you about that?"

Gabe took her hand and slipped his fingers between hers. Her hand felt so small and fragile enclosed in his, and yet he knew the power of her touch and what her hands were able to do to his body. "No, he never said anything."

"Do you think that it was on his mind when the crash happened? They said it was pilot error. Maybe it was my fault."

Gabe groaned. "Is this what you've been carrying around? Annie, it was not your fault. Accidents happen, and there's nothing we can do to stop them."

Gabe slid across the bed, making a place for her to lie down beside him. He didn't have to make a formal invitation. As soon as he did, Annie stretched out beside him, resting her chin on his chest.

"I've missed you," Annie said softly.

"And I've missed you."

"I don't like sleeping in an empty bed," she said.

He pressed a kiss to her forehead, wondering if the first brick in the wall had just fallen. "I don't either."

"Can't we go back to the way it was between us? When we were both happy?"

"I'm not sure we can," Gabe said.

She pushed up against his chest so she could look into his eyes. "Do you still love me?"

Gabe nodded. "I do. And how do you feel about me?"

"This afternoon, when I heard you'd been hurt, I felt like my heart had been ripped out of my chest. Like I couldn't breathe. Like I was drowning and I couldn't pull myself up to the surface. And I thought it was my fault. Because we fought that day." She paused, then drew a deep breath. "And for a very brief moment on the ride to the hospital, I thought I might have loved you."

"Just for a brief moment?"

Annie nodded. "Then I realized that it was probably guilt."

"Maybe it was love," Gabe suggested.

She shook her head. "If I love you and then lose you, like I lost Erik, I'm not sure I could live with myself."

"Sometimes, you have to just take a risk," Gabe said.

She nodded, then put her head back down on his chest. He didn't want to talk anymore. The more they talked, the more convinced she became that they could never be together. No, instead he just needed to touch her and hold her and make her feel safe.

Annie was such a complex creature that he hadn't figured out every little twist and turn in her personality. That could take years. But if he could just untangle a few of her worries, then maybe she could make a place for him in her life.

A soft knock sounded on the door, and a few seconds later, the physical therapist stepped inside, holding a pair of crutches. "Oh, I'm sorry. I didn't mean to disturb."

"Can we do that tomorrow? She's had a really rough day."

"Visiting hours are over at nine," the therapist said.

"I think she might be staying the night."

"Is she your wife?" the therapist asked.

"Yes," Gabe lied. "She's my wife."

"Then it's fine. We can bring pillows and blankets in for her, but she's supposed to sleep in that chair. The beds are for the patients."

She left the crutches against the wall near the door, then promised to be back in the morning around 8:00 a.m. Gabe smiled to himself as he settled back into the bed. After falling off the ladder, he'd cursed his bad luck and his lack of focus.

He had been thinking about Annie when he'd been working. But maybe it hadn't been bad fortune at all. Maybe it had been the luck he'd needed to bring her back into his life.

She was here in his bed. And she'd offered to help care for him once he got out of the hospital.

They could start again, only this time they'd begin as friends and add the benefits later. The fates had given him one last chance and he wasn't going to mess it up this time.

"YOU ARE NEVER going to be able to get from the dinghy onto the boat without falling into the water."

"So, I get a little wet," Gabe said. "I'm not going to melt."

"The doctor said you can't get your cast wet. And if you fall in, you're going to sink like a man wearing cement overshoes. You'd never be able to swim with that thing on your leg. And I couldn't save you."

Gabe had been staying with her for nearly a week, and with each day that passed, he grew more and more restless. And more irritable, as well. It had become a battle of wills to get him to rest and keep his weight off his broken leg.

He'd learned to get around with his crutches in the house and on the porch. When he ventured out on the lawn, he drove an old golf cart that her father had restored for hauling sails back and forth from the loft to the customer's cars and boats.

Out of sheer boredom, he'd taken a greater interest in the school and had taught a few navigation classes for a group of younger students.

But it was the nights that Annie feared the most. They hadn't slept together since he'd returned. He'd taken up residence in the bedroom downstairs where there was a bathroom nearby.

Late at night, she could hear him pacing, his

crutches clunking on the wood floor. Annie would lay awake, waiting to hear the sound of his footsteps on the stairs. There were some nights when she prayed that he'd make a move and visit her bed again. Other nights, she convinced herself that it was all for the better that they'd put the physical part of their relationship behind them.

"It wouldn't be impossible," Gabe said. "It would just take a little bit of effort on your part. Unless you don't want me to enjoy myself as I'm trying to regain my health."

"Well, I just happen to think you'll find a brand-new way to kill yourself. And it will be all my fault."

"Is he giving you trouble again, Annie?" One of the counselors approached, a wide grin on his face. "You know, he's tried to pay three of us to take him out there, and we've always refused. Do you have any idea how slippery it will be on deck? You'll be in the drink before you know it."

"Go away and leave me alone," Gabe said in a glum tone.

"Sit down and read a magazine," Annie said. "I'm just finishing up the dishes. We can play some cards or get out a board game. There's an Orioles game on television in about an hour."

"I hate the Orioles," he said.

"Then you can sit out here and pout like the big baby that you are."

Annie and the counselor began laughing, and that only irritated Gabe more. He turned and walked into the house, slamming the screen door behind him.

Annie looked at the counselor. "Don't you dare let him get on that boat, do you hear me?"

Annie turned and walked back inside. She expected to find him pacing the kitchen, his crutches clunking with every step he took. But he wasn't waiting for her.

She wandered through the house and found him in the guest bedroom, sprawled across the bed on his stomach, his face buried in a pillow. "Please don't put the kids on the spot like that. It isn't fair."

"Life isn't fair," Gabe grumbled. "I'm going to go crazy if I don't find something to do. I was going to start taking a few classes during the fall semester, but I can't drive. I'm stuck here for at least another six weeks until this cast comes off. Hell, I can't even go back to active duty if I wanted to."

"Not with a broken leg."

"After the cast is off, I have to have therapy and they won't let me go back until I get approved. For pilots, that's always a tricky business."

"You could get some reading done," she suggested.

He rolled over onto his back. "There is one thing we could do that would alleviate my boredom," Gabe said.

"What's that? Please. I'm starting to go a little stir crazy, too."

He sat up on the bed and grinned. "All right, then. I want you to take your clothes off while I watch."

Annie gasped. "What?"

"You heard me. Take your clothes off. I'm going to sit here and watch."

"No!" she said, shaking her head. "I'm not going to provide X-rated entertainment for you."

"Really?" Gabe said. "X-rated seems a bit overly confident, doesn't it? You're really more of a PG-type entertainer."

"You don't think I can be sexy?"

"Not that sexy," he said.

Annie knew she was being played, but it didn't matter. She had reached the end of her rope, as well. The intimate moments they'd shared were played back over and over in her head while she tried to sleep. Maybe it was time to act on those impulses.

Annie returned to the bedroom door, but instead of shutting it, she wrapped her leg around the door-jamb and slid down and then up, using it like a stripper's pole. The expression on his face was priceless.

"I usually do this with music, but you'll just have to imagine some raunchy bump and grind."

Annie moved away from the door and closed it, then bent down provocatively as she locked it with the old skeleton key. Then she pulled the front of her shorts out and dropped the key inside.

"You are naughty," he said with a chuckle.

"PG naughty?"

"I haven't seen enough to judge. Keep going."

Slowly, she removed each piece of clothing, moving around the room and allowing him tantalizing views of her body. About halfway through the strip-tease, Annie noticed that the commentary stopped and he watched her silently, the desire evident in his eyes.

They were going to indulge their desires today,

and Annie wasn't sure she wanted to do anything to stop it. She'd missed having him in her bed, and as the date of her departure approached, she was beginning to wonder if it might be nice to enjoy themselves just a few more times.

When she was finally naked, Annie walked to the foot of the bed, then crawled across the mattress until she knelt beside him. Taking his hand, she placed it on her breast, then closed her eyes and smiled.

When she felt his mouth on her nipple, she drew in a sharp breath and let the sensations wash over her. His hands skimmed over her body, touching every inch of skin as if he had to remind himself how she felt beneath his palms.

Everything happened so quickly as they rolled around on the bed, playing at seduction and laughing at the results. His cast seemed to get in the way of everything they tried to do, throwing him off balance.

Finally, she laid him on his back and unzipped his cargo shorts. His erection sprang to attention the moment the fabric parted, and he grabbed her waist and set her down on top of him.

Annie held her breath as she took in every inch of his shaft, wriggling until he was buried deep. "Now what are you going to do with me?"

He growled softly. "I think you're going to have to make all the moves."

Annie smiled, then began a lazy rhythm, rocking forward and back as she arched against him. He drew her down, burying his face between her breasts, then taking the time to tease each nipple to a hard peak.

As she gradually increased the pace, she watched his expression go from pleasure to exquisite torture. He tried to bring her along with him, but she brushed his hands away, holding his wrists on either side of his head.

She could tell he was close, and watching him resist the impulse to come was increasing her own pleasure. But she ignored the knot of tension that tightened in her core, determined to give him what he wanted.

His hands gripped her hips, and she followed his lead, driving hard and fast. And when he finally fell over the edge, he fell hard, his body jerking with deep spasms, his hips arched into hers.

He was incredible to watch, all his masculine strength and power distilled down to a few seconds of extraordinary pleasure. As she continued to move, he twisted beneath her, his body suddenly sensitive.

Gabe gripped her hips, and she enjoyed the warmth that he'd left inside her as she lay down on his chest. "How was that?"

He chuckled softly. "Definitely X-rated."

"No," she said. "That was an R. We couldn't possibly get to X with that cast on your leg. We'll need to leave that to later."

"Next time, we need to find a video camera," Gabe murmured as he toyed with a strand of her hair. "I'm going to need something to enjoy while you're off sailing the world."

"Just one video?"

"Several would be nice. Maybe a whole library."

"That sounds a bit dangerous," Annie said as she crawled out of bed. She began to gather her clothes from the floor.

"Where are you going?"

"I've got some work to do."

"You're just going to leave me here?"

Annie sat on the edge of the bed. "You can come out and help me sort the last of the gear for my next group of students. And then, if you're really good, I might let you take me out for a little row in the dinghy. And after that, I'll make you some dinner."

"You're an easy woman to love, Annie Jennings."

"And you're an easy man to seduce, Gabe Pennington." She pulled on the rest of her clothes, then gave him a quick kiss and headed out of the room. When she reached the kitchen, Annie sat at the table and cupped her chin in her palm.

Nothing had changed between them, and yet everything had. He was still in love with her, and she was finally ready to admit that she loved him. She wasn't quite sure when it had happened and had spent hours trying to pinpoint the moment. Annie suspected it was when Lisa told her that Gabe had been in an accident, the flash of terror that raced through her at the thought of losing him.

But even though the feelings were there, new and fresh and surprisingly uncomplicated, she still couldn't say the words out loud. Not yet. In two weeks, she'd say goodbye to him for six months. In that time, he'd go on with his life, free to choose another path…another woman.

But if he was there when she arrived in San Diego, waiting for her, still wanting her, then she'd know for sure. And after that, they'd begin a life together. Suddenly, she wanted to leave the next day. The sooner she was on the water, the sooner she could come home to the man she loved.

9

THE DAY OF Annie's departure dawned gray and rainy, the weather matching the mood that had descended over the little white house on the bay and held Gabe in its clutches.

The students had been gone for a week, and in that time, all traces of their presence had been stowed into boxes and bins and packed neatly for next year's school. The books had been balanced and, to Annie's relief, there was enough profit to pay the bills and the taxes.

Over the past few weeks, she'd also managed to get a few more sponsorships through *Topsail* magazine, which had added valuable resources to her budget. A line of freeze-dried meals had signed on, along with a bottled water company. And she'd received a brand-new set of sails from a top maker in the business.

Despite all the good news, Annie had been unusually quiet over the past few days, and no matter how much teasing or cajoling Gabe attempted, she could barely muster a smile. He couldn't tell if she was scared or sad, or a little bit of both.

She arranged, then rearranged everything on the boat at least two or three times, hoping to find the best balance between space and convenience. Gabe had insisted that she take more bottled water than she'd originally packed, and agreed to deleting one of the spare foresails that she'd decided to take.

"Did you check all the batteries on your emergency equipment?" Gabe asked.

She glanced up from a list she was reading. "What?"

"Batteries," he repeated. "For the emergency beacon and strobe. And for the air canister on the life raft. That needs a battery, too."

"This list just keeps getting longer and longer," Annie said. "At this rate, I'm going to be leaving in October."

"Give me that," he said. "I'll finish up with this while you go grab your foul-weather gear. With this rain and wind, you're going to need it."

She leaned in and pressed a kiss to his cheek. "Still watching out for me," Annie said.

"I'm never going to stop," he replied, dragging her into his arms. Gabe kissed her, gently at first, then with increasing passion. He kept telling himself that this was the last day they'd spend together for almost six months, but it hadn't sunk in yet. He kept expecting her to change her mind and start unpacking the boat.

But Annie showed no signs of altering her plans.

She was focused and determined, refusing to sink into periods of self-doubt or indecision. Gabe had never seen her like this, so strong and capable. She showed absolutely no weakness in the face of a huge undertaking. Hell, she ought to be the one training for NASA.

"What are you thinking about?" Annie asked, looking up into his eyes.

"I was just thinking that with your organizational skills, you ought to apply to NASA."

That brought a smile. "I don't know. That's a little risky, don't you think?"

"Riskier than sailing from here to San Diego?"

"It's not like I'm going around Cape Horn," she said. "And I'll barely be out on the open ocean. This is an easy trip."

"Excuse me if I don't agree."

"I have something for you," Annie said, reaching up to smooth her fingers across his brow. "Stop looking like the world is about to end." She left the room for a few seconds, then returned with a large vinyl envelope, the kind she kept her charts in.

Annie handed it to him and he peered inside. "This is my whole trip, planned out day by day. I'm not always going to be able to stick to this, but I'll try to call once a week so that you can know where I am and where I'll be the following week. I'm going to stop and see Lisa and Nellie. And I'm going to spend a few days with my parents in West Palm Beach. And my grandfather plans to fly into Miami and then ride along from Miami to the Keys."

"This is great," Gabe said.

"Are you going to be okay?"

He nodded. "I'm allowed to be a little sad, aren't I? After all, no more spontaneous stripteases. No more late-night skinny-dipping. No more pizza in bed."

"I'm sure you'll get along. In another month, the cast will be gone and you'll be a free man. You can go out dancing and drinking and having a fine time."

"I suspect most of my nights will be spent at home, alone, waiting for you to call. Worrying. Wondering where you might be."

"That's going to get old awfully fast," Annie said.

"Yeah, well, it's my self-pity, and I intend to wallow in it."

"This doesn't need to be a bad thing," Annie said. "I'm really excited about this trip. I've always wanted to do this, from the time I was a little kid, and now I am. You've already made your dreams come true. You fly helicopters."

Gabe knew he was being selfish. Of course he wanted her to stay. But only part of that was because he was concerned for her safety. The other part was all about his own needs. He loved having Annie with him, waking up to her each morning, falling asleep with her in his arms each night.

At least he'd have her house to remind him of the time they spent together. He planned to stay at her place until he was cleared for duty. He'd leave her sheets unwashed so he could smell the scent of her hair every night, and he'd leave a bottle of her favorite wine in the fridge and put her battered and muddy garden shoes next to the door, as if she'd come home at any minute.

He'd already snapped plenty of pictures on his phone, most of them when she wasn't looking, then chosen a number to put on his computer, as well. In truth, Gabe had done everything he could think of to make their time apart go as quickly and as smoothly as possible.

Annie stood in the center of the kitchen, her expression calm, a tiny smile curving her lips. She slowly turned in a circle, then nodded. "I'm ready," she said.

Gabe felt the knot tighten in his stomach. She'd wanted to leave at one, but it was just past eleven. He thought they'd share one last lunch together.

"Are you sure?" he asked.

A wide smile broke across her pretty face. "Yes. It's time for me to go. Right now. I can feel it."

Gabe grabbed his crutches and got to his feet, then walked over to the back door. Annie picked up a canvas bag she'd packed with drinks and snacks, then handed him the keys to the house.

"No wild parties. Make sure to keep the lawn mowed. And try to make the bed occasionally."

He gave her a quick salute. "Aye-aye, Captain."

Annie shook her head and laughed. "Argghh."

"Argghh," he replied.

They walked down to the waterfront, her hand resting on his arm, her gaze fixed on the boat floating on anchor. When they reached the dinghy, she turned to him. "I guess this is it."

He pressed his forehead against hers. "Goodbye, Annie. Fair winds and smooth sailing."

"Goodbye, Gabe. I'll see you around."

He gave her a soft, gentle kiss, cupping her face in his palms, his lips lingering over hers until he knew he couldn't delay any longer. Then he helped her into the dinghy and pushed it off the shore.

Their gazes locked for a long moment as she drifted. Then she grabbed the oars and began to maneuver herself toward the boat.

"I love you, Annie," he called, his voice echoing over the water.

"I love you, Gabe," she replied.

At first, he wasn't sure that he'd heard her right. But there was no other way to interpret what she'd said. She'd waited until the very last minute that they spent together to reveal her true feelings. And she loved him.

Gabe stood on the shore, his gaze taking in the melancholy scene before him. He watched as she stowed her things, then got the boat ready to go. They'd taken the mast down, and it was tied to the top of the cabin, where it would remain as she made her way through the Intercoastal Waterway. The bridges that crossed the waterway made it impossible to move through it for any great distance with the mast up.

The cool rain had already drenched his shirt and hair, and he brushed the damp off his cheeks, waiting for one last goodbye. Annie winched the anchor up and dragged it into place on the deck, then made her way back to the cockpit. He saw the puff of exhaust as she started the engine. A few seconds later, the sail-boat surged ahead, and she turned it in a wide circle to head south, toward the mouth of the bay.

She waved to him as she passed by, then threw him a kiss that he pretended to catch. "Safe journey," Gabe murmured to himself as he waved back.

He'd waited years to have a chance with Annie, and they'd found happiness together. But now she was leaving, and though he wanted to believe that everything would be the same when she returned, Gabe wasn't naive.

Absence didn't always make the heart grow fonder. But if Annie loved him like she said she did, then he had every reason to hope that they'd be together at the end of her trip…and for the rest of their lives.

BY THE TIME Thanksgiving rolled around, the *Honey-moon* was anchored in the beautiful blue waters off the coast of Belize. After sailing from Jamaica straight to Cancun, Annie found her confidence in single-handing. The weather had been good, without a single threat from hurricanes, and the boat had been operating without a hitch.

As she sliced a mango for her lunch, she looked out at the small harbor, searching the flags that each boat flew to designate its home country. There were at least four or five American flags and a couple Ca-nadian flags.

The family in the sixty-foot sloop had invited her for Thanksgiving dinner, along with the rest of the Americans anchored in the harbor. Tomorrow, they'd all make their way over to the boat to enjoy a locally grown turkey and the traditional side dishes. Annie had promised to bring the wine, as she had packed much more than she'd ever have time to drink.

As promised, she'd called home once a week, using the satellite phone that Gabe had bought her. Their conversations were always longer than they should be, considering the ridiculous rates, but Gabe wasn't concerned about the money.

Though she'd brought her laptop along, she'd limited herself to using it just once a week, when she sent in her copy for her column in *Topsail* magazine and when she retrieved emails from her account. It was always a sketchy affair, making sure the battery was charged off the boat's engine, then finding an internet café with Wi-Fi before the battery ran down again.

Gabe had written her every day, keeping her up-to-date with the details of his life. But his last few emails brought unwanted news. He'd been medically cleared to return to duty, but since he still had two months before his assignment to test pilot's school, he was being sent back to Afghanistan.

He'd accepted the orders without complaint. In fact, he'd been anxious to get back into the air again and reunite with the guys in his unit. But for Annie, the thought of him walking back into a war zone frightened her. Had she been at home, she would have tried to talk him out of going, encouraged him to find a way out.

But Gabe had always put duty to his country before everything else in his life, and now, that included her.

She'd thought about leaving the boat at a marina and flying home to see him before he left, but she was already on a thin budget, and the expense of going through the Panama Canal was looming in the next few weeks.

Annie took a bite of the mango, then licked the juice off her fingers. She could always call him. He wasn't scheduled to ship out until next week, and though this wasn't her regular night for a call, she wanted to hear his voice anyway.

She grabbed the sat phone from the cabin and brought it out onto the deck, then sat down beneath the sun shade that she'd draped over the cockpit. With sticky fingers, she punched in his phone number.

Her heart began to flutter as she waited for him to pick up. He always kept his cell phone on, knowing that she might call, but this time it rang and rang and he didn't pick up. Finally, Annie turned the phone off, then wondered if she ought to try Lisa and Nellie.

The two of them had promised to keep in touch with Gabe while she was gone. Certainly, they would know whether his orders had been changed. She dialed in Lisa's cell phone and waited as it rang, but like Gabe's, there was no answer.

"Where is everyone?" she murmured.

Suddenly, she felt completely alone in the world. Annie was surprised by the intensity of emotion, the depth of loneliness that overwhelmed her all at once. Tears swam in her eyes, and with a soft laugh, she brushed them away.

It was probably the holidays that had brought out

the tears, Annie mused. Everyone was back home, enjoying Thanksgiving together, and she was here, eating mangos and getting ready to celebrate with a bunch of strangers.

"Stop feeling sorry for yourself, Annie Jennings. You're on the greatest adventure of your life. Hundreds of people would give their left arm to do what you're doing. So stop whining and suck it up."

She'd been gone nearly three months, and in that time, she'd learned so much about herself, about a strength she never knew she possessed. There were moments on the water when everything seemed to go wrong at once, when a confluence of bad weather, broken equipment and loneliness converged to make her absolutely miserable from morning until night.

But Annie had learned to pick herself up and get back to the business at hand. She'd learned to put aside her emotions and deal with challenges one at a time. She allowed herself some time to feel sorry for her solitude, but never more than ten or fifteen minutes every few days.

She'd also come to the conclusion that she was in love with Gabe and had been for much longer than she was willing to admit. The pinpoint had moved back from his injury to the moment when he danced with her at Lisa and Nellie's wedding. As far as she was concerned, fate had put him into her path and they'd been meant for each other all along.

"Ahoy, the *Honeymoon*!"

Annie looked over the gunwale to see a rubber dinghy approach with a devastatingly handsome Swede at the controls. She'd met Gunnar yesterday right after she'd dropped anchor and learned that he was also headed to the West Coast through the canal.

"Hello," she called, sending him a bright smile.

"I heard you talking to yourself," Gunnar said in perfect English. His Swedish accent was barely detectable.

"You did?"

"You know what they say. Once you start talking to yourself, you won't be able to stop."

"Do you talk to yourself?" Annie asked.

"Of course I do," he said. "I'm a brilliant conversationalist. There's no one else I'd rather talk to."

Annie laughed. It was nice to have a handsome man pay attention to her. "Can I help you with something, or did you just come over here to warn me about my one-way conversation."

"Actually, the Johnstons invited me to their Thanksgiving tomorrow and asked if I'd bring something to add to the feast. I was hoping you might have a recipe or two that I can borrow."

"I'm just taking wine," Annie said.

"I'd like to cook something. But I don't know anything about Thanksgiving."

Annie grabbed the line from his dinghy and invited him on board. Though the ache of loneliness was still there inside her, at least she could distract herself for a while.

"I have a dish you could make. You can get yams and brown sugar and butter at the local market. And

I have a bag of marshmallows. You could make candied yams. That's a very traditional dish."

"Yams," he said. "And marshmallows."

"Do you know what marshmallows are?" Annie asked.

"Of course. I went to college in America. They're little puffy things that you melt in hot chocolate."

"Right. Well, when you put them on top of sweet potatoes, they're heaven." Annie jumped up and grabbed a pen and paper from the cabin, along with the bag of marshmallows.

She handed them to Gunnar and opened the bag and popped a handful in his mouth. "Ewww," he said. "They're just sugar."

"What did you expect?" Annie asked, laughing.

She spent the next hour teaching Gunnar about the various Thanksgiving customs that she usually observed, and he seemed to be a captivated student. But Annie could tell that he was interested in more than just conversation. In fact, she'd met a lot of single men cruising the Caribbean who were available for brief flirtations and casual sex.

No doubt Gunnar could have his pick of the ladies, but Annie didn't intend to be one of them. She had a man waiting for her at home. At least she thought she did.

When Gunnar got up to leave, Annie was careful to maintain a physical distance between them. But it was no use. He stepped closer and gave her a kiss on both cheeks, then moved in to kiss her lips.

Annie didn't stop him, but when his tongue tested

the crease of her mouth, she drew back and smiled. "I'll see you tomorrow," she said.

"Thanksgiving," Gunnar said.

Annie nodded and waved as he drove off in the dinghy, the small outboard engine carrying it smoothly through the harbor.

She cleaned up the cockpit and then headed down into the cabin. It had been a long day, and she was exhausted. Tomorrow was a holiday, and she'd wait to try Gabe again. Tomorrow was a holiday and they'd talk as long as they wanted. She needed him to fill an empty spot in her heart, a spot that threatened to get bigger if she tried to ignore it. A spot that no other man could fill.

GABE GRABBED THE strap of his duffel and hoisted it over his shoulder, then stepped away from the battered old bus that had brought him to the seaside village in Belize. He'd been traveling for nearly twenty-four hours, bouncing from airport to airport and then taxi to bus, until he found himself at his destination.

The trip to see Annie hadn't been planned, but after he got his orders to return to Afghanistan for the two months before his new assignment, he decided that he wasn't going to set foot in a war zone until he'd had a chance to be with her once more.

He knew exactly where she was and that she planned to spend the Thanksgiving holiday with some Americans she'd met. So all he had hoped for was a trip without any delays. He glanced at his watch. It was 6:00 p.m. local time, and Annie should be exactly where she said she would be, on a sixty-foot sloop with a family called the Johnstons from Cape May, New Jersey.

He walked down to the waterfront and scanned the boats in the harbor, looking for the familiar blue hull and silver mast of the *Honeymoon*. He caught sight of the boat, bobbing on its anchor, but after watching it for a long moment, he realized that it didn't look like she was aboard.

He heard laughter coming from another boat, a large sloop that had been tied off to one of the docks, and decided to wander over and inquire about Annie. At least she was still in the marina, that much was certain.

Gabe reached into his pocket and held the small velvet box between his fingers. He'd bought the ring months ago, right after Annie had invited him to stay in the apartment above the boathouse.

He'd considered it an act of faith, a sign that he'd do anything and everything to make it work with her. There had been times when he wondered if buying the ring had been bad luck, especially when things fell apart between them. But Gabe was ready to take the chance, ready to know if she really meant what she said as she sailed away from him.

Her words still echoed in his brain. *I love you, Gabe.* So simple, yet powerful enough for him to want to change his life forever.

He'd leave his life as a combat pilot behind once he headed to the test pilot's program in February. He'd also work on a doctorate through Johns Hopkins in Baltimore. The next few years would be busier than usual, but Gabe was looking forward to starting a new career path.

As he walked down the dock, he heard a familiar laugh, the sound echoing over the water. He turned his attention to a sixty-foot sloop anchored near the *Honeymoon*. A large group of people had gathered in the cockpit and were enjoying a meal together.

Gabe squinted against the late-afternoon sun, searching for a glimpse of Annie. She was sitting near the stern, facing him. A handsome man sat beside her, his arm thrown over the back of her chair. They seemed to be deep in conversation.

Gabe watched them both for a long minute, trying to make sense of what was going on. The man seemed to be captivated by her, but Annie wasn't giving him much encouragement. Every time he tried to engage her in conversation, she'd give him a quick answer and then turn back to the others at the table.

Gabe glanced around for a dinghy he could borrow or rent, but he couldn't find anything available. He thought about walking back to the harbormaster's hut near the gate, then decided against it. Instead, he set his duffel down at the end of the pier, then kicked off his boat shoes and stripped out of his shirt.

The casual cargo pants he wore wouldn't weigh him down too much. He zipped the ring into a pocket before diving off the pier and heading out into the harbor toward the elegant cruiser.

No one heard him approach, but when he grabbed

the swim ladder and crawled on board, the conversation stopped immediately. He appeared over the stern of the boat, dripping water from his cargo pants, which clung to his lower body like a second skin. His gaze caught Annie's and she gasped.

"Gabe?"

He grinned. "Hi, Annie."

"Oh, my God. Gabe!" She scrambled out of her seat and jumped onto the deck, circled the cockpit and leaped up onto the stern. Gabe wasn't prepared for the intensity of their embrace. She flew into his arms, knocking him off balance.

She screamed as they both fell into the water. Gabe cupped her face in his hands and gave her a long, deep kiss before drawing back to look into her eyes. "God, you look good. Look at your hair. It's so blond."

"What are you doing here? How did you get here? How long have you been here?"

"I came because I had to see you, and you don't want to know what it took to get here."

"How long can you stay?"

"A week. I can catch a military transport out of Honduras next Friday. But until then, I'm all yours."

She kissed him again, once on the lips, then raining kisses over his cheeks and eyes. "I was just thinking about you yesterday. I was so lonely I was wondering what it would take to go home to see you. And now you're here."

"Would you like to come back on board and dry off?" someone called from the boat.

"Actually, we're good," Annie said, kicking away

from the boat. "I think we'll just swim back to my boat."

"All right, then," Mike Johnston said. "But if you'd like to come back later for dessert, you're welcome."

"Thank you for the invitation," Gabe said.

"Thank you," Annie called.

They swam the short distance to the *Honeymoon*, then Gabe helped Annie crawl on board. He followed her up the ladder, then grabbed her from behind and picked her up off her feet.

"Do you have any idea how much I missed you?"

"Not half as much as I missed you," Annie said.

"Are you having fun?" Gabe asked.

Annie nodded. "Although I really wished you were here with me. There are so many wonderful things to see and do, and I wanted to share them all with you."

"There's something I want to share with you," Gabe said.

He reached inside his pants pocket and retrieved the blue velvet box. It dripped water as he opened it and held it out to her. Annie's eyes grew wide as she looked down at the box, the diamond sparkling in the late-afternoon light.

"What is that?" Annie asked.

"You know what it is," he said with a grin. "Do you think you may want to marry me someday?"

"Someday?"

"I'm not going to be hanging out in any war zones in the near future."

"I thought they were going to send you back until February," Annie said.

"They were. But I guess I'm needed at Pax River. They've decided I'll stay there until I start test pilot's school in February. After that, graduate school and then NASA. Or maybe I'll take that teaching job at the academy. I don't know that the future holds for us, but I know that I want to spend it with you."

"It's a beautiful ring," she said. Annie thought about it for a long moment, then shook her head. "I can't do it."

Gabe's heart stopped. "You can't?"

"I can't make you leave the military, Gabe. I can't put conditions on our feelings for each other. I was wrong to do that. And if you want to continue to fly, then that's up to you, too. I'll love you no matter what you decide to do."

Gabe held out the box to her. "Marry me, Annie."

"When?" she asked.

He began to laugh. "I don't know. We'll have to work out all the details."

"Do you think we can find someone to marry us down here?"

"You want to get married this week?"

Annie nodded. "I do. I don't want you going back home without me married to you. You might meet some beautiful woman who wants to steal your heart."

"All right," Gabe said. "Now take the ring."

"No, you have to put it on me. Get down on one knee. There's a way this is done."

Gabe did as he was told, pulling the ring out of the box and rolling it between his fingers. "I'm going to ask once more, and if you don't say yes this time,

I'm going to throw you in the water. Annie, you're the woman for me. I've waited all these years for you, and I don't want to wait a moment longer. Will you marry me?"

Annie nodded. "Yes, Gabe. I will marry you."

She threw herself into his arms and kissed him. From across the harbor they heard cheering and applause and turned to find the crowd on the Johnstons' boat standing and celebrating with them.

Annie wrapped her arm around his waist and hugged him tightly, then waved at her new friends.

"Who is that guy you were sitting next to at dinner?" Gabe asked.

"Oh, that's Gunnar. He's from Sweden."

"Do I have any reason to worry about him?"

Annie glanced up at him and shook her head. "Nope. No reason at all. I'm pretty sure he was looking for some of that friends with benefits action, but I only do that with one guy."

"We're not just friends anymore," Gabe said.

"But we were friends first," Annie said. "And then lovers. And soon we'll be spouses. And lifelong partners. I think maybe we've always belonged together. It just took us a little while to find each other."

Gabe gathered her into his arms and kissed her, bringing another round of cheers from the nearby boat. "I think we should take this down below," he said.

"Aye-aye, Captain," Annie replied.

* * * * *

If you enjoyed this novel, look for previous Harlequin Blaze titles from Kate Hoffmann, available now!

SEDUCING THE MARINE
COMPROMISING POSITIONS
THE MIGHTY QUINNS: THOM
THE MIGHTY QUINNS: TRISTAN
THE MIGHTY QUINNS: JAMIE

Harlequin is thrilled to announce
the launch of a new sexy, contemporary
digital-only series in January 2018!
With the exciting launch of this new
series, June 2017 will be the last month of
publication for Harlequin® Blaze® books.

For more passionate stories, indulge in these fun,
sexy reads with the irresistible heroes you can't
get enough of!

HARLEQUIN

Presents®

Glamorous international settings…
powerful men…passionate romances.

HARLEQUIN

Desire

Powerful heroes…scandalous secrets…
burning desires.

HBEND0617

If you enjoy passionate stories from Harlequin® Blaze®, you will love Harlequin® Presents!

Do you want alpha males, decadent glamour and jet-set lifestyles? Step into the sensational, sophisticated world of Harlequin® Presents, where sinfully tempting heroes ignite a fierce and wickedly irresistible passion!

Look for eight new stories every month!
Recommended Read for July 2017

Maisey Yates The Prince's Captive Virgin Ruthless prince Adam Katsaros offers Belle a deal—he'll release her father if she becomes his mistress! Adam's gaze awakens a heated desire in Belle. Her innocent beauty might redeem his royal reputation—but can she tame the beast inside?

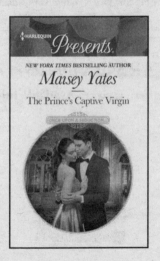

Look out for The Secret Billionaires trilogy from Harlequin® Presents!

Three extraordinary men accept the challenge of leaving their billionaire lifestyles behind. But in *Salazar's One-Night Heir* by Jennifer Hayward, Alejandro must also seek revenge for a decades-old injustice…

Tycoon Alejandro Salazar will take any opportunity to expose the Hargrove family's crime against his—including accepting a challenge to pose as their stable groom! His goal in sight, Alejandro cannot allow himself to be distracted by the gorgeous Hargrove heiress…

Her family must pay, yet Alejandro can't resist innocent Cecily's fiery passion. And when their one night of bliss results in an unexpected pregnancy, Alejandro will legitimize his heir and restore his family's honor…by binding Cecily to him with a diamond ring!

Don't miss

The Secret Billionaires
SALAZAR'S ONE-NIGHT HEIR

by Jennifer Hayward Available July 2017!

"You're offering to buy my baby? Are you out of your
mind?"

"I'm giving you the opportunity to make a fresh start."

"Without my baby?"

"A baby will tie you down. I can give this child everything
it needs," Ariston said, deliberately allowing his gaze to drift
around the dingy little room. "You cannot."

"Oh, but that's where you're wrong, Ariston," Keeley
said, her hands clenching. "You might have all the houses
and yachts and servants in the world, but you have a great
big hole where your heart should be—and therefore you're
incapable of giving this child the thing it needs more than
anything else!"

"Which is?"

"Love!"

Ariston felt his body stiffen. He loved his brother
and once he'd loved his mother, but he was aware of his
limitations. No, he didn't do the big showy emotion he

suspected she was talking about, and why should he, when he knew the brutal heartache it could cause? Yet something told him that trying to defend his own position was pointless. She would fight for this child, he realized. She would fight with all the strength she possessed, and that was going to complicate things. Did she imagine he was going to accept what she'd just told him and play no part in it? Politely dole out payments and have sporadic weekend meetings with his own flesh and blood? Or worse, no meetings at all? He met the green blaze of her eyes.

"So you won't give this baby up and neither will I," he said softly. "Which means that the only solution is for me to marry you."

He saw the shock and horror on her face.

"But I don't want to marry you! It wouldn't work, Ariston—on so many levels. You must realize that. Me, as the wife of an autocratic control freak who doesn't even like me? I don't think so."

"It wasn't a question," he said silkily. "It was a statement. It's not a case of if you will marry me, Keeley—just when."

"You're mad," she breathed.

He shook his head. "Just determined to get what is rightfully mine. So why not consider what I've said, and sleep on it and I'll return tomorrow at noon for your answer—when you've calmed down. But I'm warning you now, Keeley—that if you are willful enough to try to refuse me, or if you make some foolish attempt to run away and escape—" he paused and looked straight into her eyes "—I will find you and drag you through every court in the land to get what is rightfully mine."

Don't miss
THE PREGNANT KAVAKOS BRIDE
available July 2017 wherever
Harlequin Presents® books and ebooks are sold.

www.Harlequin.com

Turn your love of reading into rewards you'll love with
Harlequin My Rewards

**Join for FREE today at
www.HarlequinMyRewards.com**

Earn **FREE BOOKS** of your choice.

Experience **EXCLUSIVE OFFERS** and contests.

Enjoy **BOOK RECOMMENDATIONS**
selected just for you.

PLUS! Sign up now
and get **500** points
right away!

Earn
FREE
REWARDS
HarlequinMyRewards.com
Join
Today!

MYR16R

HARLEQUIN®

A *Romance* FOR EVERY MOOD™

Love the Harlequin book you just read?

Your opinion matters.

Review this book on your favorite book site, review site, blog or your own social media properties and share your opinion with other readers!

Be sure to connect with us at:
Harlequin.com/Newsletters
Facebook.com/HarlequinBooks
Twitter.com/HarlequinBooks